Emma Donoghue is an Irish novelist, playwright and historian who lives in Canada. Her other books include *Room*, *Passions Between Women*, *Stirfry*, *Hood*, *Kissing the Witch*, *We Are Michael Field* and *Slammerkin*.

The Woman Who Gave Birth to Rabbits

Emma Donoghue

virago

VIRAGO

First published in Great Britain by Virago Press 2002

9 11 13 15 17 19 20 18 16 14 12 10 8

Copyright © Emma Donoghue 2002

'A Short Story', 'Figures of Speech', and 'Night Vision' were
broadcast on BBC Radio 4 in June 2000, 'Words for Things' was
first published in *The Penguin Book of Lesbian Short Stories* (1993), 'How a Lady Dies' in *Hers
3* (2000), 'The Fox on the Line' in *Circa 2000* (2000), and 'Looking for Petronilla' in *The
Vintage Book of International Lesbian Fiction* (2000). 'A Short Story' was included in a
limited-edition calendar by Language in Dublin (2001), and 'Figures of
Speech' was first published in *The Lady* (2001).
I am grateful to Peggy Reynolds for being the first to suggest I should write a historical short
story, and also to Eddi Reader, because I conceived this book all at once
during an enspiring concert of hers in Cambridge.

The moral right of the author has been asserted.

A CIP catalogue record for this book
is available from the British Library.

ISBN 978-1-86049-954-8

Typeset in Times by Palimpsest Book Production Limited,
Polmont, Stirlingshire
Printed and bound in Great Britain by
Clays Ltd, St Ives plc

Papers used by Virago are from well-managed forests
and other responsible sources.

MIX
Paper from
responsible sources
FSC
www.fsc.org   FSC® C104740

Virago Press
An imprint of
Little, Brown Book Group
Carmelite House
50 Victoria Embankment
London EC4Y 0DZ

An Hachette UK Company
www.hachette.co.uk

www.virago.co.uk

This book is dedicated with love
to my father, Denis,
who taught me that books are for letting us
imagine lives other than our own.

Contents

Contents

Foreword

The Woman Who Gave Birth to Rabbits is a book of fictions, but they are also true. Over the last ten years, I have often stumbled over a scrap of history so fascinating that I had to stop whatever I was doing and write a story about it. My sources are the flotsam and jetsam of the last seven hundred years of British and Irish life: surgical case-notes; trial records; a plague ballad; theological pamphlets; a painting of two girls in a garden; an articulated skeleton. Some of the characters in this collection have famous names; others were written off as cripples, children, half-breeds, freaks and nobodies. *The Woman Who Gave Birth to Rabbits* is named for Mary Toft, who in 1726 managed to convince half England that she had done just that.

So this book is what I have to show for ten years of sporadic grave-robbing, ferreting out forgotten puzzles and peculiar incidents, asking 'What really happened?', but also, 'What if?' In her novel *Les Guérillères* (1969), published the year I was born, Monique Wittig urges: 'Try to remember, or, failing that, invent.' I have tried to use memory and invention together, like two hands engaged in the same muddy work of digging up the past.

The Last Rabbit

We were at home in Godalming, though some call it Godlyman, and I can't tell which is right, I say it the same way my mother said it. I was pregnant again, and cutting up a rabbit for our dinner. I don't know what sort of whim took hold of me to give a scare to my husband, that is Joshua Toft. When he came in from his day's work at Will Parson the stockinger's, I leant on the stool and huffed like a bellows. ''Tis my time come early, Joshua,' I told him.

Now, he was all set to run for his sister but I reached up and grabbed hold of his shoulders and bore down with a great groan that must have woken the children behind the wall. Then I reached under my skirt and what did I pull out but the skinned rabbit, with the dust of the floor stuck to it in places?

Joshua staggered till his back hit the wall. I thought he might spew up his breakfast.

Then I took pity on the man and started to laugh. I laughed more than I had in many a year.

We amused ourselves very much with talking of it till we went to bed. Joshua said I was a clever one and no mistake. When his sister came in the day after to borrow a drop of milk, we told her all about it and she laughed very hearty too. She is a midwife, like her mother, and has often said no man could bear what women must.

1

I miscarried of that baby some weeks after, while I was shovelling dung on the common. It was just as well, Joshua said, as in these times we were hard put to it to feed the two we had got already. The cloth trade was gone quite slack, and Joshua had no work nor any prospects.

'Mary,' my sister Toft (Joshua's sister, that is) said to me, 'look at that rabbit.'

She and I were out in the hop field off the Ockford Road, weeding at tuppence a day; I was still bleeding, but stronger in myself. There was a fat rabbit watching us. 'Too far off to catch,' I said.

'Mind that trick you played on poor Joshua, though.'

I straightened up and smiled a little.

'Think how it would be if it was true,' she said. 'If you was the first woman in the world to give birth to a rabbit. Wouldn't that be a fine thing?' She had let her trowel fall on the clods. 'If it was true, Mary, would you not soon be famous? Would people not pay to see you? We would all be in the way of getting a very good livelihood, and not have to scratch it out of the ground.'

My husband's sister is a good woman, but given to mad notions. 'How could it be true, though?' I said, bending to the weeds again.

Her eyes were shining now. 'Weren't there a child born a few years back with dog's feet, because the woman was frighted by a dog in her sixth month? And another only last year born with all its organs on the outside, that I myself paid a penny for a look of?'

I tried to speak but there was no stopping her.

'And if who can tell what's true and what's not in these times, Mary, why then mayn't this rabbit story be as true as anything else?'

I do not think as quick as my sister Toft but I come to the point in the end. 'I'll not go round to fairs, but,' I told her.

'No need, no need,' she said, picking up her trowel again. 'The folks will come to you.'

It was said of Mr Howard the man-midwife that he'd drop his breeches in the High Street of Guildford if it would increase his fame. Before he put his hand up my petticoat to see was I big enough for the trick we were planning, I sent the children to stand outside, though it was raining. The doctor's hands were as cold as carrots, but Joshua bade me hold still. Mr Howard said it was all to the good that I still bled, off and on, after miscarrying, and had a drop of milk in my breasts; it would be more lifelike, that way. If all went well and I won some fame, he said, the King might give me a pension in the end.

Now, I couldn't see why I'd get a pension for bringing forth rabbits, when the country was full of them already, but Mr Howard was an educated man.

Joshua got some dead rabbits from Ned Costen and some from Mary Peytoe and some from John Sweetapple the Quaker, all at thruppence a head; no more than three from anyone, so as not to cause wonder. From Dick Stedman the weaver he got a very small grey one at tuppence. We kept them piled up in the cool of the cellar. I caught our girl playing with one and smacked her legs.

I wiped a space on our table for Mr Howard's paper and ink and pen. The letters he composed were full of grand words: *The woman Mary Toft has just now given birth to five praeternatural rabbits, all dead, a fact of which there is hitherto no instance in Nature.* He pickled them in my sister Toft's jelly jars, numbered one, two, three, four, five, just as they were supposed to have come out of my womb. All I had to do was produce one more out of my body in front of a crowd of London doctors, and they would all believe in it. 'Stupidity and knavery, that's what we can rely on,' said Mr Howard, wiping his hands on a rag.

3

But nobody came, for all his letters.

After a week Mr Howard ran over from the inn with a notion that he would teach me to make my belly jump as if live creatures were sporting in it, which would be all the more impressive. Our children thought it a great game. Mr Howard sent off more letters. *The woman Mary Toft has just now given birth to three more rabbits, one of which leaped in her body for all to see, for eighteen hours before it died and came out, which was a great satisfaction to the curious.*

But the weeks went by, and still nobody came to see me.

When Mr Howard knocked on our door, with a long face, I thought the game was over, and I was not sorry neither, though he might have given me a shilling for my trouble. But instead he said I must go in his chaise to Guildford, which would be more convenient for him to carry on the scheme.

At this I began to be afraid, but Joshua got out of bed and said I must go. His brother's wife could come in and see to the children, as she had none left of her own.

'What sport,' said my sister Toft, who was to come with me as my nurse.

Mr Howard kept writing letters all the way, though the ruts splashed ink on his lace cuff. *There are three more rabbits come out of the woman Mary Toft's body, the sum being eleven, all which may be seen in jars at Guildford by any person of distinction who likes.*

While he was resting his hand, I asked him, 'How many rabbits, sir, could one woman of middling size be supposed to have in her body?'

But he said they were only small ones, and eleven was a good number.

I lay on the bed in Guildford and groaned and made my stomach go in and out so the sheets moved, just as I was instructed.

4

I had to keep my eyes shut so as not to laugh. Some folks came in to see me at last. One pointed and said she could see the shape of a rabbit's paw, but her husband said it was clearly a tail. Others only stared, and one woman said it was a fraud and spat on the floor. Mr Howard wouldn't charge any of them so much as a farthing. 'Patience,' he told my sister Toft, 'our sights are set higher.'

Joshua came to Guildford on Nat Tucker's cart one day. He told me I was a good woman, then lifted the lid of his basket a crack so I could smell the fresh rabbits he had brought.

'Is it not a great expense,' I said in his ear, 'when we could be feeding them to our children?'

But he shook his head, lightsome as ever, and said soon we would have the King's coin and dine on venison.

The morning I heard the jangle of a gentleman's carriage out in the courtyard, I felt so cold in my bones that I would have run all the way home to Godalming, if Mr Howard had let me out the door.

I was to look weary and say little; that was easy. I kept my stays on, but loosened. The visitor was a foreign gentleman, a Mr St Andre, surgeon to the King himself. He felt my belly and remarked that it was barely swollen. Then he reached into my dress and squeezed my nipples to see what would come out.

Mr Howard ran back from the inn at dinner time, with sauce down his neckerchief, and told me not to fret. 'St Andre is no man-midwife, Mary; the only females he's seen close up are dead ones.'

At that I started to shudder, but my sister Toft told me to give over my nonsense.

That afternoon I gave birth to my first rabbit, which was supposed to be my twelfth. The first thing was, Mr St Andre rolled up his flowing cuff and put his hand into me, to be sure there was nothing there. He turned his face from me and stared at the wall. After I had moaned and shifted about a while, Mr Howard walked me up and down the room. In the darkest corner he sat me down on a stool opposite him, and squeezed my legs between his own. Mr St Andre called for a light, but my sister Toft cried out that it would hurt my eyes. All this time I kept up my panting and wailing. Mr Howard took my hands in his and squeezed them. He leaned his head against mine. Then he pushed me back all at once, as if the creatures were leaping inside me, so my stool almost toppled. Mr St Andre came closer, but Mr Howard told him sharply to sit down again, so an unfamiliar face would not disturb the woman at her moment of crisis.

Now I could feel Mr Howard reaching under my skirt in the shadows, and taking the limp rabbit from my pocket that dangled inside my hoop. He kept talking as if to soothe me while he nudged my legs apart and pushed the creature into me. I slid forward on my stool to help him; tears were falling down into my stays. It felt like cold cheese, till a little bone scraped me.

Then Mr Howard had me walk about the room again, to bring on the birth. I kept my steps small, so it would not slide out. Mr St Andre's eyes were on me no matter which way I turned, and I felt like a tumbler who has used up all her tricks. I tried to remember what it was like, the times my real children were born. I leaned on the back of a chair, squalling and roaring and twisting my body from side to side. I told Mr Howard I thought I might be ready, but he frowned and had me lie down on the bed for another while. My sister Toft wiped my face with vinegar.

The two doctors passed the time by means of jokes. When Mr Howard told a good one about a sow I couldn't help but join in the laughing. Mr St Andre looked at me oddly and I shut my mouth. 'Ah, women of Mary's station are hardy as beasts, sir,'

Mr Howard told him. 'They don't recall a hurt when it's over.'

At that I began to roar again, as if the pains were doubled. The doctors ran to the bed. I pushed and pushed so my eyes bulged; I could feel the mangled rabbit beginning to slide out.

'There,' said Mr Howard, 'can't you hear its little bones crack?' The men listened, not meeting each other's eyes.

Mr St Andre shook back his three rows of lace to the elbow before he reached into me. The rabbit came out on the first tug. It lay in his hand, the skin hanging loose. We all stared at it. My sister Toft muttered something like a prayer. It was dry and bloodless. It didn't look much like a rabbit.

'In the cases of several of the others, also,' Mr Howard said very fast, 'the public bone crushed the foetus and the skin was pulled off in its passage through the *os uteri*.'

Mr St Andre's wig had slipped sideways. He adjusted it, and wrote everything down in his little memorandum book. Prompted by Mr Howard, I told him how my sister Toft and I had been weeding in the fields one day, and I saw rabbits and had a great desire for them, and tried to catch them for my pot, but could not, and that night dreamed I had rabbits in my lap. (And indeed, by now, it was true, I did dream of rabbits most nights.)

'What is the pain like, Mrs Toft?' he asked.

I thought back to the birth of my boy, two years past. 'As if very coarse brown paper is tearing inside me, sir.'

He kept feeling my pulse, looking at my tongue, even examining the water in my pot for stains. He did all this without ever saying if he believed a word of our story. He took three of the pickled rabbits away with him, to dissect in front of the King.

I heard Mr Howard standing by the carriage, reminding Mr St Andre to tell the King what pains he, Mr Howard, had taken with this poor woman, and how he did not debar her from eating anything she fancied, no matter what it cost. And it was true, I

7

suppose, that when there were no visitors I was free as any woman to sit by the fire and eat salt beef and drink strong beer as good as the doctor himself. The one thing I might not do was go home to my children, though I didn't trust my husband's relative to feed them. Mr Howard shouted that he had staked his whole reputation on that magical womb of mine, and I was to get back to bed.

In the days after, a Mr D'Anteny came down from London, and a Mr Ahlers and a Mr Molyneux and a Mr Brand, and other doctors whose names I forgot as soon as I heard them. They all carried three-cornered hats that would never fit over their wigs. There was much nodding and bowing to each other, but anyone could have guessed they were not friends.

They watched me like owls. I am not a handsome woman; all my features are bigger than they need be for a body so small. But these gentlemen looked at me as if I was made of gold, and by now I was so brazen I could look right back. One wiped his hand on his satin breeches and said he had discovered an enormous great tumour in the woman's – meaning, my – stomach, but Mr Howard informed him that it was simply the neck of the womb. He didn't like that, to have his ignorance made a show of.

The births we performed late in the afternoon, when it was too dark to see clearly but not so dark that the candles had been brought in. Mr Ahlers pulled out the fifteenth rabbit like a child digging for treasure. 'Did I hurt you?' he asked.

'Yes, sir.'

And he wrote it down in his book, and gave me a guinea, for my misfortunes.

Mr Howard laughed, later, and said he'd wager I never got a guinea for a rabbit before. But his voice was high in his throat, and his hands were restless; I could tell he was fretting.

8

The visitors would not deny this rabbit miracle, nor swear to it. Two of the doctors spoke foreign gibberish; the others only hummed and hawed, and refused to make so bold, and could not positively say, and deferred to their learned friends' opinions. The day I produced my eighteenth rabbit, I suddenly saw what my sister Toft had meant, when she told me how impossibilities might as easily be believed as not.

I was sore inside from strainings and pokings, and bled more than I had before. I couldn't sleep at night for visions of fields full of rabbits. One day the lodging-keeper tried serving me one for dinner, and I spat it out. She complained that her larder was choked with rabbits, and that throughout the country, as no one was willing to eat what might have come from between a woman's legs. My sister Toft roared laughing and told me I was famous.

I couldn't laugh. Did I know, by then, that our luck was running dry?

All I remember is that when the maid announced Sir Richard Manningham the next day, the first sight of him filled me with dread. He was a man-midwife, they said, who knew more about childbirth than anyone living.

'The *os uteri* is so tightly shut,' he murmured as he pulled his smooth hand out of me, 'that it would not admit so much as a bodkin.'

I shrank from him.

Sir Richard pointed out that my belly was flat, and said the leaping motion was merely a muscular spasm. I lay still, panting. I knew his dark eyes could see right through me. My sister Toft gave me sneezing powder, to dislodge the rabbits, she said. I sneezed till my nose bled. Sir Richard lent me a handkerchief. I started to cry.

'Why do you weep?' Sir Richard asked me, not unkindly.

9

My sister Toft told him it was no wonder the poor woman cried, when he had as good as called her a liar in front of the whole company.

The room grew hotter; sweat ran down my sides. The air was thick with breathing. I asked for a window to be opened, but Mr Howard said night air would be fatal in my condition. Instead he let me have some more beer. I began to hate him.

I tried to remember if childbirth itself was as bad as this mockery of it. With my last boy I was three days in labour, but at least I knew there was a real child to bring forth, not like this hollowness, this straining over nothing.

The doctors spent hours in the inn; I could hear their quarrel from across the road.

The end of it was, I had to go to London with Sir Richard Manningham. I never thought of going to London before; folk said it was full of rogues that'd steal the skin off your feet. But I was not given a choice. So I took my guinea that Mr Ahlers gave me, though Joshua would have rathered I left it at home, and my sister Toft said I should not forget she was entitled to her cut of the guinea and the pension too, after I met the King. I was terrified when I heard that Mr Howard was not to come to London with myself and my sister Toft and Sir Richard, but he did lean in the carriage window and tell me my reward could not be far off. He seemed so full of the story, now, he almost believed it.

We lodged at a sort of bathhouse in Leicester-Fields. I was locked in my room at all times, and kept without my shoes, and nursed by a stranger with a flat face. When I asked for my sister Toft, Sir Richard said she was kept downstairs, and there she must stay.

One might have thought Sir Richard was my father, or my lover, so tirelessly did he sit up all night watching over me, and writing down everything I said or did. I complained of the most

10

peculiar pains; I fell into fits. My acting grew more desperate, like a strolling player trying to be heard over a crowd. I curled up my fingers, rolled my eyes, and whined like something dying in a trap.

All the time my mind was sniffing out ways of getting hold of a rabbit. Just one more, that's all I needed. Just a part of one even, as little as a furry foot, for luck.

One day when Sir Richard had stepped out for a moment's air, the porter came in with some mutton for my dinner. I talked sweetly to him, and mentioned I had an aversion to mutton, and begged him to tell my sister Toft in the kitchen to send up a rabbit for my dinner.

The porter let out a great guffaw and asked what he would get for it. I had no change, so I had to give him my guinea.

Sir Richard stalked in later. I could tell by his face the porter had betrayed me to him.

I sobbed. I said, 'I had such a strange craving to eat rabbit, sir, because I am big with one still.'

He was staring at me, and I could not tell if it was with triumph or disappointment. 'You are big with nothing but lies,' he said, very low. He examined me once more. His hands on my legs were so familiar, they almost felt safe. But then he said to me, 'Mary Toft, I have prevailed upon the Justice not to send you to prison yet, but to keep you in custody here, until the full story emerges, that we can only see the tip of now.'

I groaned and clawed at the bed like a woman in the throes of death. Sir Richard's eyes were sad. I realised then that, for all his suspicions, he half-wanted to be wrong. I would have been so glad to have brought out one last rabbit, to let it fall like a holy miracle into his fine hands.

Towards evening I fell into a real fit and lost all conscious-ness of who or where I was. When I woke up my face was as

11

hot as a coal and there were cramps in my belly like the grip of fingernails. My lies had infected me, I supposed. My counterfeit pains had come true.

Sir Richard came in, then, with a case under his arm.

'I have a fever,' I told him, very hoarsely.

He ignored that. He opened his case so I could see what was inside. There was a scissors, a forceps, a hook, a crotchet, a small noose, a saw, and various knives, with other instruments I didn't know the names of. The points and blades caught the firelight.

I thought I was going to vomit.

'I have come to the conclusion, Mary Toft, that you are a fraud.' Sir Richard spoke in a soft voice, almost gentle. 'Either you make a full confession of how you have imposed upon the whole medical establishment of England with your motions and your pains – in which case I will attempt to have your sentence reduced – or else I must here and now put you to a painful experiment to see how you are made different from other women, that you have managed to convey into your uterus what should not be there.'

The fever had dried up my voice; it came out as a croak. 'Sir, for mercy's sake, give me one more night.'

He rubbed his eyes wearily. He spoke more like an ordinary man. 'What, girl, can the conjurer at every fair bring a rabbit out of a hat, and you cannot produce one more from between your legs, when you claim to have brought forth so many already?'

I clutched my belly. 'It is there, sir. I feel it stir and press, but it can't find its way out.' And then I put my face in my hands and it felt like a burning thing. 'Sir,' I said, 'I won't stay here any longer. I'd sooner hang myself.'

Sir Richard said he would give me one more hour to consider the state of my soul. Then he locked the door on me.

But for a month I had been nothing but a body. Though I believed that every body had a soul, as my mother taught me, I

12

had no idea where it might reside. How could there be anything hiding in me that had not been turned inside out already?

The crack of the bolts. Not Sir Richard, but the unsmiling nurse, with a leg of chicken for my supper.

I gave her one great shove and ran past her, out the door and down one corridor and then another.

My breath ran out soon enough; my head hammered like an army. I had to stop and lean against a wall for weakness. I hadn't my guinea any more, I remembered, nor my shoes even; what would become of me?

I heard laughter from one of the chambers. The door was open a crack, and I peered in. There was a sofa, and a girl lying on it, with her skirts up to her shoulders, and an old man kneeling between her legs, his back heaving as he thrust. Now I knew what kind of a place this so-called bathhouse was. I couldn't help but watch for a moment. I never saw a man and a woman do what they are born to do, except for Joshua and myself, and that I never looked at from outside. The girl's eyes were shut; I could tell she was used to it. It came to me then that it is the way of the world for a woman's legs to be open, whether for begetting or bearing or the finding out of secrets.

I looked up the corridor, then down. I knew I would never find the way out on my own. So I turned and walked back to the room where Sir Richard was waiting for my story.

Note

For 'The Last Rabbit', which was inspired by William Hogarth's famous engraving of Mary Toft (1703–63) giving birth, I have drawn on many contradictory medical treatises, witness statements, pamphlets and poems, including Nathaniel St Andre, *A Short Narrative of an Extraordinary Delivery of Rabbets* (1726); Cyriacus Ahlers, *Some Observations Concerning the Woman of Godlyman in Surrey* (1726); Sir Richard Manningham, *An Exact Diary, of what was Observ'd during a Close Attendance upon Mary Toft* (1726); *The Several Depositions of Edward Costen, Richard Stedman, John Sweetapple, Mary Peytoe, Elizabeth Mason and Mary Costen* (1727); and 'Lemuel Gulliver' [pseud.], *The Anatomist Dissected* (1727).

Dr Howard was charged with conspiracy, and Mary Toft was sent to the Bridewell jail as a 'Notorious and Vile Cheat', but she was released after a few months, probably to save the prominent Londoners taken in by the hoax from further embarrassment. Back in Godalming with her husband, Mary had another baby in 1728 ('the first child after her pretended rabbett-breeding', according to the parish register), and was occasionally shown off as a novelty at local dinners. In 1740 she was charged and acquitted of receiving stolen fowl, and she lived to the age of sixty.

Acts of Union

The young captain was stationed in Ballina, in that part of Mayo where the French invaders and the Irish rebels had triumphed so briefly during the recent troubles of 1798. These days, ever since the Act of Union had come into law, the countryside was quiet enough. All that was troubling the young captain, as he rode over the narrow bridge to Ardnaree, was a nasty sore.

'It's on my, ah, manhood,' he muttered to the apothecary, whose name was Knox. 'My *membrum virile*, don't you know.'

'We call a prick a prick in this country, sir,' said Knox pleasantly. 'A rash too, all over? Yes, yes, I've seen this many a time before. And what part of England did you say you hail from?'

The captain hadn't said; but he did now. It was hard to refuse information to a man who was holding one's penis between finger and thumb, and peering at it through greasy spectacles. The captain told the whole short story of his career to date, and when he had finished the apothecary gave him an old claret bottle full of black liquid, stoppered with a rag. 'Nothing to worry about,' said Knox. 'Three swigs of that every morning, and wash yourself in the same stuff at night.'

The bill, scribbled on the back of an old militia notice, staggered the young captain.

15

'Why, but I'm not charging you a farthing for my own humble services; it's the medicine that costs, my boy,' Knox told him. 'I admit it, you'd be cheaper dipping your wick in frankincense and myrrh! Though I venture to predict they wouldn't do the trick in the case of this little problem like my patent mercurial tincture will. Good air, regular sleep and evacuations, and riding too,' he added. 'You'll be your own man again by the time you get back to your good lady in England.'

The captain was not married.

'Is that so?' asked Knox, and invited him to stay for dinner and try a fine pink salmon caught in the Moy, 'off the very bridge you crossed this morning. Famous for its fish, our river, if I say it as shouldn't.'

They ate in a parlour of such smoky darkness that the captain could barely distinguish his plate. With the soup ladle, Knox proudly pointed out a framed licence from the Worshipful Company of Apothecaries up in Dublin, but the captain could hardly make out a word of the spidery print. 'I'm no mere druggist, you understand, sir,' Knox assured him. 'My profession is a genteel one, no matter what some high-and-mighty physician might tell you. I'm the best you'll find in this part of Mayo for bleedings, purgings, plasters or any other cure. Yet some of my ignorant countrymen take their ails to the farrier instead, can you credit it?'

The visitor laughed politely, and tried not to scratch his rash.

The other guests were a skinny little parson and an attorney from Ballina. They talked politics from the start – meaning to impress him, he could tell.

'Oh, we suffered in Mayo during the late troubles, let me tell you, Captain,' sighed Knox through his soup.

The attorney was nodding along. 'Those craven Wexfordmen, they hadn't half as much to bear. The rebels stole a flitch of bacon from my own kitchen!'

16

'And then the crown soldiers confiscated my whole stock of bandages and all my French brandy besides,' complained Knox.

'There was a rumour going round, at the time,' said the parson in a thrilling voice, 'that every man, woman and child of us would be gutted with a pike if we didn't convert to Rome.'

'Aye, we were in fear of our lives, all through the fighting. Blood flowed down the streets of Ballina,' said the attorney.

'And Ardnaree,' murmured Knox.

'It did not,' said the attorney, helping himself to more port.

'It did so.'

'The battle took place in Ballina,' raged the attorney. 'Isn't that right, Reverend? Wasn't it through the streets of Ballina that the Frog soldiers and their papist traitor underlings pursued us with pistol and sword?'

The parson nodded, speechless as he gnawed on a rabbit bone he had found in his soup.

'Nobody pursued you anywhere, sir,' said Knox; 'you were locked up safe in your parlour.'

The attorney ignored that remark. 'So how, may I ask, did those rivers of good Protestant blood cross the bridge to Ardnaree and flow *up* the street, contrary to the law of gravity?'

'It's a figure of speech.' Knox rolled his eyes. 'You should have stayed longer in school.'

The young captain laughed nervously, and coughed on a piece of gristle, and choked. Knox ran round the table to thump him on the back. When the captain could breathe again, his host beamed down at him and told him he was a lucky fellow not to lie dead in his plate. 'And I won't charge you a penny for that little service, either!'

The fish was brought in and carved by a woman to whom nobody seemed to pay much attention. The captain found himself glancing sideways at her, every now and then; despite the dark

17

fug of the room, he could see that she had pale hair in a tight bun, pale eyes, and shadowy crescents under them. Finally she drew up a stool.

The fish was sweet, flaking in his mouth. 'Most excellent salmon, may I say,' the captain told the woman, and she gave a brief nod.

The attorney was expounding on the multitudinous benefits of the recent Union. 'Ireland now shelters in the protective embrace of Britain, to their great mutual advantage.'

'If only every Irishman saw it that way,' sighed the parson.

'I was told,' said the young captain, stopping to clear his throat, 'my superiors informed me on arrival, that is, that the rebels had been quite put down in this part of the country?'

'Well, yes,' said Knox blandly, 'but there'll always be troublemakers.'

'Those who protest at paying tithes to God's own Established Church,' complained the parson.

'And the occasional hamstringing of cattle, as a consequence of evictions. Secret societies, and the like,' contributed the attorney.

'I see,' said the captain, pushing a bit of fish-skin round his plate in a disconcerted manner.

'As a crown soldier, you should mind your back, on dark nights, hereabouts,' said the parson with relish.

'And your throat!' Knox went off in a long guffaw.

The captain met the eyes of the woman, who shook her head a little as if to say they were only teasing him. She seemed weary, listless; her shoulders sloped, hiding her body from view.

'You like the look of my niece, young sir?' Knox called down the table.

The captain flinched, and looked away.

18

'You're not the first, nor will you be the last.'

'Oh, aye?' said the attorney, with a titter.

The host gave his friend a belt on the shoulder. 'Shush, you. How're your piles these days, by the way?'

'Very bad,' said the attorney, sheepish.

'I'll roll you some more pills. And laudanum, that's your only man for the pain.'

'I need another few bottles too, for my stomach,' the parson put in.

'I'll send them over with Seán in the morning. But as you were saying, Captain, my niece is a treasure,' he said, turning back to the visitor, 'a prize beyond price, beyond rubies, as they say in the Good Book.'

Miss Knox's eyes never lifted from the platter of roast beef which she was carving. Her fingers were very slim.

'Helps my lady wife run the household, so she does, not to mention sewing and spinning and all manner of feminine accomplishments, isn't that right, lassie?'

She gave her uncle a brief, unreadable look.

'You'll put her to the blush,' said the parson.

'Oh, nonsense,' said Knox, 'the dear girl must know her own worth.'

'I do,' she said, very quietly, and the young captain almost jumped in his seat, to hear her speak at last.

'Twenty-three years old, merely, and the wisdom of a grandmother!' boasted her uncle.

The captain said he did not doubt it.

The attorney whispered something in the parson's ear.

A little later, Knox burped, clapped his hands for the plates to be taken away and the bottles to be brought out. 'You'll take a dram with us, young man.' When he caught sight of his niece slipping out the door he bellowed out 'Miss! You'll not deny us

19

the favour of your company tonight. Set yourself down there, in the empty chair.'

She slid on to the seat beside the Englishman, blank-faced.

'She's only shy, don't mind her,' her uncle assured the captain. 'A little prey to melancholia, ever since she lost her parents, and she's not the only one whose spirits are depressed in these troubled times. I'm dosing her with salts; she'll be lively as a doe come summertime.'

The captain smiled at Miss Knox. He wondered what it would take to make her smile. Kinder treatment than she got from these rough old men. Sympathy and sensitivity, from someone who understood the finer feelings of the soul.

'Will you have some parliament whiskey,' the attorney was asking the young visitor, 'or will you take some of the good stuff?'

He looked confused.

'Poteen, don't you know,' contributed the parson in a loud whisper; 'there's not a hill in Mayo without a few stills speckled across it! Sure, on this land, few could pay the rent without the cash it makes them, and the landlords know it.'

'Half the price of the taxed stuff,' commented Knox, 'and besides, *stolen water is sweetest*, as the proverb tells us.'

'Mayo poteen, now, is nearly as good as the Donegal, which is agreed to be the best, especially if it's from Inishowen,' the attorney told the captain.

'I beg to differ. Mayo's better by far,' said the parson hotly.

'Maybe our guest will take a dram of both,' suggested Knox.

'Parliament whiskey and Mayo poteen, or Inishowen?' demanded the attorney.

'All three, for a true comparison,' decided Knox.

The first hit of poteen shook the young captain like a dog. 'My God,' he coughed. 'I heard the rebels were mad with drink, by the time the French landed; was it this stuff they were on?'

'Not at all,' said Knox in outrage; 'it was Scotch whisky they'd looted from some squire's cellar. Poisonous stuff!'

The second toast was to the King, and the third to the Union; the captain could hardly refuse. He couldn't tell the Inishowen from the Mayo poteen, no matter how many times his host made him try; he lacked an Irishman's palette. When the young man attempted to pass on the bottle, next time around, the parson took offence. 'Didn't Jesus himself drink wine with his friends?'

'No sober man's long welcome in Ireland. Don't tell us you're on milk and tar-water, for your health!' said the attorney in amusement.

'He is not,' said Knox, topping the visitor's glass up; 'nary a bit of harm a drop of the cup that cheers will do him.'

An hour later the captain felt like the conqueror of the world. The room swam around him. He saw kindness on every man's face. Miss Knox's white throat seemed to him to be like a swan's. She sipped a small glass of poteen, and kept her eyes on the table. He felt he knew the shadowy thoughts of her melancholic mind, the secret motions of her bosom.

'I think the lady likes our young Englishman,' said the attorney with a grin.

'I think she does! There are certain unmistakable signs, to a trained medical eye. And sure what lady wouldn't,' said Knox, slapping the captain on the nearest shoulder. 'The young are drawn to each other, as natural as magnets.'

The parson proposed a toast to young love.

The attorney followed it up with a toast to young lovers, naming no names, wink wink.

'How well I remember my own dear departed wife, your aunt,' said Knox, with a nod in his niece's direction, 'on the day I met her, and her barely home from school in Dublin. Ah, marriage,' he extemporised, 'that shelter from every storm, that medicine for every ill, that cornucopia of delights!'

'I tell you this much,' the attorney breathed heavily in the captain's ear, 'if you were to make your proposals to young Miss Knox there, this very night, I don't think you'd be shown the door!'

The captain let out a shriek of laughter. 'Do you think not?' he whispered back. 'I mean, do you think so?'

The attorney threw his arm round the visitor. 'Hem, hem,' he said loudly, chiming his fork against his glass. 'Our young visitor has something to say.'

In the long silence, the captain felt panic bubble up in his head. He threw Miss Knox a wild glance. 'Oh no,' he stuttered, 'I was just saying, I mean . . .'

'What the young gentleman in question was wondering,' said the attorney, 'was whether our generous host would ever consider . . . surrendering his lovely niece?'

Knox threw up his hands in delight. The woman shot to her feet, but her uncle had a hold of her wrist. He pulled her down again, bent over her as if in an embrace, whispered fondly in her ear for some time.

The captain watched, frozen. He didn't know what he hoped or dreaded. His vision was blurred; his head was a burning bush.

'Fear not, my boy,' hissed the parson.

When Knox sat down again, his niece's face was very still. He spoke with a calm grin. 'In answer to your question, my dear young sir, I believe I'll follow modern custom and let the lady answer for herself.'

She turned her head to the captain; her milk-white face was only inches from his. She nodded, just once.

A cheer went up from the three older men.

'You do me the greatest honour, Miss Knox,' the captain babbled, and took another long swig of poteen to steady himself.

'We could wed next week, perhaps, at St Michael's in Ballina.'

'Sure what need a moment's delay, when Providence has so arranged it that we've the holy vicar of St Michael's sitting here across the table?' said Knox, pointing with an air of wonder. 'He could do it right this minute. It's the Irish custom, you see,' he explained, 'to marry at home.'

'Tonight?' faltered the captain. 'But—' He turned towards Miss Knox.

Her uncle creased his brow and put the question to the attorney. 'Here we have two young Protestant persons of sound mind, past the age of majority – it'd be legal enough, surely?'

'Indeed, indeed so.' The attorney nodded over his glass.

'Let's do it, then,' said Knox, leaping to his feet and tugging open a bureau drawer. 'You can draft them a simple contract; here's a clean sheet of paper. Of course,' he threw in the captain's direction, 'the poor sweet girl is dowerless, and I couldn't rob my own, but as the poet once said, *Do phósfainn* – hey, how does it go?'

He appealed to the attorney, who recited sonorously,

> *Do phósfainn-se gan feoirling thú*
> *Is ní iarrfainn ba ná spré*

'Beautiful,' sighed Knox.

'Is that Gaelic? What does it mean?' asked the captain, bewildered.

'*I'd wed you without a farthing, and ask no cow nor dowry*,' Knox translated. 'Such a noble and timeless sentiment! Tell you what,' he added suddenly, 'tell you what I'll do, I'll pay the marriage dues out of my own pocket this minute.'

'That's very handsome of you, Knox,' said the parson.

'No bother. Sure don't I love the girl like my own? Start

23

up now, Reverend, now's as good a time as any. "*Do you, etc. . . .*"'

At a gesture from her uncle, Miss Knox stood up. The captain clambered to his feet beside her. He couldn't stop giggling; his cheeks were hot. He had never thought to be married before tonight. It was all so fast, so funny, so unexpected, and yet, as the apothecary said, so clearly destined by Providence.

The parson said no more than a few fluent lines. The groom hiccuped in the middle of his *I do*, but the words came out clearly enough. The bride murmured her answer without moving her lips. He was too drunk and excited to read the contract; it looked well enough. Their signatures on the bottom of the page almost touched.

'I give you a toast, now,' Knox roared, when the brief ceremony was over. 'To a most glorious union between two young persons, two families, two nations under God!'

In the morning light the young captain thought his head would crack open. He was lying in a strange room, sunken into a very bad mattress. There was a dark shape, a woman sitting on the edge of the bed, with her back to him. He remembered now. He leaned the other way, tugged the chamber pot towards him, and threw up violently, spattering the floor. 'Pray excuse me,' he gasped. He wiped his mouth with the back of his hand. And remembered the rest of it.

She turned her white face to him, and it was traced with faint lines around the eyes, around the down-turned mouth.

'You're not twenty-three.' In his wretchedness, it was all he could think to say.

'I am thirty-four years old.' Her voice was low, but clear.

'What's your name? I don't know your name, even!'

She watched him coolly.

'I was drunk. I was poisoned with that foul poteen,' he ranted. 'I didn't know what I was doing. I only rode over from Ballina yesterday for some medicine.' He bent and scrabbled for his clothes on the floor. 'That was no valid wedding!'

'You gave your consent. There was a parson,' she added, 'and an attorney.'

'Oh, how damnably convenient! Does your uncle invite that pair to dinner every night, just in case a suitor for his spinster niece might ride by?' And then as the young captain heard himself say those words, the truth hit him. He looked into the back of her pale eyes. 'It was a trap.'

She did not deny it.

'Knox only sent for his friends once he knew I was staying for dinner. An innocent stranger who might be tricked into taking a burden off his hands! The parson to wed us and the attorney to call it legal. You were all in league against me from the first mouthful of soup.'

'Not I,' she said austerely.

He slammed his hand on the mattress. 'What in hell d'ye mean, *not I*?'

'I was not party to the plan.'

'Weren't you desperate to get your claws into me the minute I rode up to the door? Isn't every spinster hungry for a husband?'

She narrowed her eyes to slits. 'I'd have to be a deal hungrier before I'd take you. If you think', she spat, 'that I'd give a farthing for a pox-ridden Englishman—'

He blinked at her. 'What? It's not—'

'It's syphilis you've got,' she told him flatly. 'If Knox told you not to worry, he was lying. In the end, it'll rot your balls, and then your brain.'

He wanted to throw up again, but he was empty.

'Maybe your brain's rotted already. You still don't understand,

25

do you?' She spoke with a cold impatience. 'The only reason I took part in that charade of a ceremony was because my uncle told me this was me last chance, and if I refused, I'd never sleep another night under his roof.'

The captain took a moment to absorb this. 'You could have said no, even so,' he raged at her. 'Surely you could always find work – spinning, even—'

'Tuppence.' Her arms were folded. 'Tuppence a day, that's what a woman makes by spinning. So don't tell me what I should or shouldn't have done, Captain.'

He stared at his bride for some time. Finally he spoke in a hoarse whisper. 'What have we done?'

One of her faint eyebrows lifted. 'Nothing much,' she said.

'I absolve you of blame,' he told her. 'I admit you're as much your uncle's victim as I am.'

Her eyes were cool.

'If I've, if it turns out that I've infected you, I beg your pardon,' he said, knowing he sounded like a boy. Then a dreadful thought occurred to him. 'And if there should be other consequences – a child – I'll make provision—'

For a moment her face relaxed, and sweetened, and she laughed.

The young captain blinked at her.

'There'll be no consequences,' she told him. 'Nothing happened, if that's what's worrying you. I sat here all night and listened to your snoring. We've never so much as shaken hands.'

He should have felt relieved. He got off the bed. As he was pulling on his regimentals, he wondered why a weight still hung on him. 'I'll go, then.'

She nodded, indifferent.

'I expect to be posted back home shortly.'

26

She nodded again.

'I'll never speak of this to anyone,' he said, tugging on his boots. 'And I'll make this bargain with you,' turning to her, 'if you agree never to claim me as your husband – never kick up any fuss, or come to England—'

'What would take me to England?'

'Well, if you promise not to, I'll send you an allowance every year. Not much, now,' he added nervously, 'but perhaps enough to give you a little independence.'

Miss Knox considered the matter, her eyes lidded. 'I'll be a sort of widow,' she said at last.

'That's right. Only, if you should ever wish to remarry—'

'I won't.' Her face was as set as a statue's.

He didn't understand this woman, but on an impulse he held out his hand. 'Until we meet again?'

'I think we never will.' His hand was starting to tremble by the time she shook it.

Downstairs, the servants claimed that Mr Knox was out attending to a dying man in Killala, and wouldn't be home all day. This time the young captain knew he was being lied to; he thought he would always recognise the sound of it, from now on. He got on his horse and set off back to Ballina. His head pounded like a drum in battle. He looked over his shoulder once, at the window of the room where he had spent the night, but there was no face at the glass.

Note

'Acts of Union' is based on an anecdote about two unnamed people – a niece of an Ardnaree apothecary called Mr Knox, and a visiting stranger – in *Elizabeth Ham, by Herself* (written in the 1840s, published 1945). Elizabeth Ham, an English writer, was living in Ardnaree around 1810 when she saw Knox's niece, and heard the gossip about her. According to Ham, the husband went on to become Aide-de-Camp to a Royal Duke, and never saw his bride again.

The Fox on the Line

Any other June, we would be in Hengwrt by now. I would be waking up with the white-topped mountains ringed around me. Cader Idris, where the giant once sat, would raise its stony shoulder between me and all harm. Sitting under the snowy cherry tree I would keep one ear cocked for the brook that sounds so much like a woman singing, you have to lay down your book and go and see.

But we are trapped in London, waiting to make history.

Keeping a diary is a monstrous waste of time. But I cannot seem to help it. Without words, we move through life as mute as the animals. Of course I burn these jottings at the end of each year. What I should keep instead is a daily memorandum of my dearest Fà and all her works. Posterity will not interest itself in me; I am only her friend. Her Mary.

On the first of June 1876, then, our Society commenced business with a General Meeting at the Westminster Palace Hotel, Lord Shaftesbury presiding, myself (Miss Mary Lloyd) taking minutes. Cardinal Manning defied the Pope and spoke in our favour. Fà (Miss Frances Power Cobbe, I should say) eloquently proposed a resolution in support of our Bill, which was passed with the utmost enthusiasm.

I break off here to remark that it cannot go on, the evil, I mean. We spill their blood like water. There is so much we could learn from them – devotion, patience, the fidelity that asks no questions. The men of science say they pick only the useless ones, but who is to decide that? And what are we to think, we old maids who have so often heard ourselves called *surplus*?

It stands to reason that those who assault Nature will suffer at her hands in the end. I read these stories every other day in *The Times*. A boy was beating a plough-horse with the stock of his gun. The gun backfired and took his arm off.

Do I sound uncharitable?

It has been a long year.

Every week, our Bill creeps a little further through the House, progressing like a pilgrim under the flag of Lord Carnarvon. I try to steady my heart. I work a little every morning in my sculpture studio at the bottom of the garden. My hopes shoot up and down like a barometer. But we walk by the Thames when the sky has begun to cool, and Fà ends each evening by convincing me all over again. The great sacrifice she made last year, when she laid down all her other causes and writings, will be rewarded at last. Every newspaper supports our Bill. The Queen is reported to be most impressed by its wording.

In the veterinary schools they reckon on sixty operations for each horse before it is used up or dies of its own accord. The professors set students to do things that have been done a thousand times before, that could as easily be done on corpses. They practise finding nerves. They burn the living horses, make them breathe smoke and drink spirits, pull out their guts, carve off their hooves, pluck out their eyes, peel back their skin. Still living. If that can be called living. My hand shakes on the chisel when I think of it.

Fà has on her bedroom wall a text that her great-grandfather the magistrate had on his. *Deliver him that is oppressed from the hand of the adversary.*

I am attempting a cocker spaniel in brown marble. My master when I trained in Rome was John Gibson – a Welshman, but a Greek in soul. He always encouraged me to be mythological, and I did once try a Niobe, but the swell of her marble breast disconcerted me. I cannot believe in anything I have not seen. All I make these days are dogs and horses.

Kitty brings the letters to me as soon as they arrive, so I can remove the hateful ones. I can tell by the handwriting. They call Fà a stirrer-up of sentimental old women, despite the fact that there are rational people of both sexes in our campaign. If they only knew how little of an extremist she is; she laughs at faddy vegetarians and hunt protestors. All she means to do is control a necessary evil – to minimise pain, to make the men of science accountable. They call her a squeamish coward, but where is the courage in what the vivisectors do? Boys pulling wings off flies.

The day our Bill becomes law, no experiment whatsoever may be performed on a living cat, dog, horse, ass or mule, nor on any other animal except (in almost all cases) under conditions of complete anaesthesia from beginning to end. The reign of terror is almost over.

I wish we were in Wales. It is easier to believe in a state of nature there.

No news.

Last year Fà and I passed through the Vale of Llangollen and visited the pretty house where the Ladies lived. It is said the two of them never slept a night away from home. Nothing parted

31

them; nothing disturbed them. They supported no causes. They took no part in public life. They did nothing; they were ladies in the old sense. They looked no further than the ends of their aristocratic noses.

Shall I confess? Sometimes I long for such a life. A narrow, private existence, as Fà would call it; a limited life. House and hearth and daily bread. Like Rosa Bonheur and her friend, when we visited, with their horses, goats, sheep, monkeys, donkeys, lapwings and hoopoes! I can imagine us at Hengwrt with our animals around us, well fed and tended, and no thought of all the others. No memory of all the viciousness of the world.

Fifteen years ago we made our bargain. A trip to Wales every summer, but Kensington all the rest of the year. Meetings, dinners, petitions, debates, dinners, appeals, circulars, dinners, calls, printings, meetings, dinners. There are things to be said on platforms; things to be said at tea tables. And things not to be said at all.

A lady lion-tamer put her head in a lion's mouth, last week, and he bit it off. If a lion attempted to put his head in my mouth I expect I would do the same.

Lord Carnarvon has been called away from London to his dying mother. She lingers; he has been gone for a fortnight now. Meanwhile our Bill lacks a midwife to see it through the House. Fà rages at Carnarvon for what she calls his dereliction of duty. But how is the poor man to choose? On one side, the muffled cries of hundreds of thousands of creatures; on the other, his mother. It would drive anybody mad.

The slightest things set us a-jitter, at this eleventh hour. On the way home from chapel I panicked at the bray of an ass. Yesterday I snapped at Fà over the grocer's bill. She asked if I would prefer her to earn a thousand a year or do God's work on earth?

If we cannot love each other through times like these, then what we thought a rock beneath us is turned to shifting sands.

She was on crutches when I met her. Summer in Rome; I was working on a model of my little Arab horse when Charlotte Cushman was announced, with a visitor. To think of a time when it was not familiar, that warm bulk, lurching across the room! An Irish lady of honourable birth, Miss Frances Power Cobbe. She told me very cheerfully about the doctor who had left her crippled. I asked her to come riding on the Campagna. I was merely being polite; I never thought she would come.

She wrote me poems which were very bad but softened my heart. She boasted that not only had no man ever wanted her but that she had never wanted any man. She said that love was the highest law, and that the Bedouins had rites to solemnise the mutual adoption of friends.

I went home with her three years later. I took her to Wales. She said 'Hang the doctors,' and threw away her crutches, and we climbed Cader Idris.

If I shut my eyes I am in Hengwrt in our dark-panelled dining room, our little Rembrandt girl looking down at us with serious eyes. It cannot be long now. I have sent word that half a dozen rooms should be aired for our arrival.

I chip away at my spaniel, but it lies awkwardly on its marble rug.

Fà is shut up all day with lords and bishops and men of influence. I must order a good beef stew for dinner.

I remember Hattie Hosmer in her smock and cap, climbing the scaffolding around one of her giantesses. 'Art or marriage, Mary,' she used to remark, 'it's one or the other.'

* * *

33

Still no news.

I lost my temper twice this afternoon, though I kept my lips together and Fà never noticed. Would she like me better if I were a dumb beast?

We try to stick to our routines. We are always in bed by eleven o'clock. We have few friends, these days. Half are lost to us because of bitter arguments over the cause. Even our beloved Harriet St Leger looked up from brushing her great black retriever and remarked that she could not understand us. 'My dear girls, a dog's just a dog!'

But she is wrong. A dog, pinned down in a laboratory, its nostrils full of the stink of phenol and its own blood, is more than a dog. It is the whole sin of our race in miniature.

Nowadays I see vivisections everywhere. In the heels that deform women's feet, for instance; in the corsets that grip our lungs. 'If we dress like slaves,' Fà says, 'no wonder men enslave us.' I have known two women who died of having their ovaries removed, quite unnecessarily. I have heard whispers of another fashionable operation, where a part is cut away that is not diseased at all. The surgeons do it simply to kill passion. Simply to make women quieter. Simply because they can.

Three thousand doctors and scientists have signed a Memorial to the Home Secretary, protesting at the insult we do their professions by attempting to subject them to legal control. They propose amendments to every word in our Bill. A crowd of them marched into the Home Office and slapped it on the desk.

Fà got to the letters before me this morning. She cried when she read one accusing her of wearing a feather in her hat that was ripped from a living ostrich. Such an absurdity! A woman who for half a century has worn only the plainest home-made suits. I made her laugh about it, over caraway cake. I called her a slave to fashion.

Does she guess? Does she see through me? The truth is that I long for this Bill to pass not so much for the animals' sake as for ours. For this battle to be over, and the two of us come safe home.

I read in *The Times* about a fox who saved his own skin. A pack of hounds was on his heels when he suddenly turned in the direction of the railway, and lay down on the line. An express was approaching at a fearsome speed. Unwilling to see their hounds cut in pieces, the huntsmen had to call off the pack. The fox stayed on the track until the train got within ten paces, then slipped off into the countryside.

Knowing when to go, that's the trick of it.

No word from Lords Carnarvon or Shaftesbury. No news of the Bill. July has come in dank and windy. Fà is irritable as always when bad weather keeps her home; like a dog, she needs her constitutionals.

I have been addressing letters all morning; my hand is a claw. I have copied out Fà's table of arguments and rebuttals till I am heartily sick of them all and can no longer remember which ones I am meant to believe. I dread the next meeting of our Society, the motions and counter-motions, the pompous, desperate repetitions. Perhaps I will pretend to have taken a chill.

What am I doing here, in the anteroom of a public life? I was born to live tucked away in a quiet green corner of the world, with my stones and my chisels, under the long rocky shoulder of Cader Idris. That is my true habitat. If I had known my own mind fifteen years ago – if I had met and joined my life to a different kind of woman—

I will burn this page before dinner.

As the poem goes, *I have looked coolly on my what and why*.

Because when Fà is away mending the world she writes to

35

me every evening, and keeps every letter I ever sent her in a big box.

Because greed for cake is her besetting sin.

Because she lumbers along precipices and laughs at the drop.

Because her head, as measured by a skilled phrenologist, is twenty-three and one quarter inches in circumference.

Because nothing quells her. When she heard that Ruskin called her a clattering saucepan, she roared, 'The better to boil his head down to size!'

Because she thinks every girl should be taught how to hit a nail straight.

Because she is such a bright light that no one peers behind her at me.

Justice and Mercy have gone from the earth.

The Bill has been read in the Commons. We barely recognise it. It has had its throat cut, the life blood drained out of its veins. It is a shadow of itself now, a mockery, a twitching monster.

It no longer protects animals from vivisection, but vivisectors from prosecution. It allows anyone to apply for a licence to do anything to any animal. It says a man of science is under no obligation to put a suffering creature (such as a blinded rabbit or an eviscerated rat) out of its misery unless in his opinion that suffering is likely to endure long.

Fà leaned against me, when the news came, and her whole weight bore down. 'Mary,' she said, 'what have we done?'

At times like this I wish we shared a bed, as some friends I knew in Rome used to do. Then I could hold her all night. Fà has always joked about her body, calling it Kensington's own grotesque. She doesn't understand that I love every pound of flesh.

*   *   *

Late August, and we are in Wales. The Parliamentary Session is over, and the summer, and all our hope.

The Vivisector's Charter is passed. It is the first time I have ever cursed the Queen. We always thought Victoria was on the side of the animals; we always said she had a tender heart. How could she have signed her name to this?

Hengwrt does not seem as beautiful as it was last summer; we have missed the best of it. Or rather, all its loveliness is at a little distance, as if behind glass. The Rembrandt girl's eyes puzzle over us.

Fà never looks up. She is busy writing the bitterest letters I have ever read, to those of our supporters who have melted away. I have begun again on the business of circulars. I print them and post them and eminent people sign them and return them and I compile a list of the signatories and send it to other eminent people. Circular is the right word.

The damage is done, but we go on; nerves are cut, but still they feel. An unpopular cause has its own momentum. It bears down on you, blind and urgent as a train. Qualms are no longer permitted. We have set our faces the way we mean to go. There is no more room for nice distinctions, reservations, doubts, normal life.

Another story for my scrapbook. An old man went hunting rabbits with a ferret, and was found buried days later, halfway up a collapsed burrow.

Of course, saving them may kill us too.

Lord Shaftesbury writes to say that the Act is better than nothing, and should be given a chance. Mr Gladstone assures us, again, that his sympathies are with us – but will sign nothing.

Some we once called comrades have given in entirely. We burn their letters. Why waste our breath pleading for reform? We will

37

settle for nothing now but abolition. Government is corrupt. Doctors and scientists are liars, all. We will address ourselves to the hearts of the public with a simple message. No living thing should be cut open to satisfy human curiosity.

I say we, because I am as one with Fà in this.

I persuaded her to spend the afternoon in the garden, for the good of her health. The shrubs are dreadfully overgrown. She cuts the best flowers to send away to the friends we have left. I hold the basket and she wields the knife like a sabre.

This evening I looked at my plate and felt queasy. Now I begin to consider the claims of the animals afresh, it seems to me that vivisection is only the outermost skin of the onion. Whatever about the rest of Mr Darwin's views, he has proved that we are closer to the lower kingdoms than we ever suspected. God has made us all of one stuff. And I wonder now why, if Fà and I will not fish for sport, on principle, we still dine on salmon? Why I sit here in boots made of calfskin, holding a tortoiseshell comb, on cushions filled with down, on a horsehair stool?

These thoughts make me dizzy. I have not mentioned them to Fà; she would tell me I was getting hysterical.

But where does it end? We have fenced in the creatures of the world, made them depend on us like fearful children. We cannot seem to live without their labour, their milk, their skins. What would it mean to tear up this dreadful contract? How could we begin all over again?

From Fà's window you can see the little churchyard where, in time, we will lie together. Our souls, I hope, will be in a better place. *They shall not hurt nor destroy in all my holy mountain, saith the Lord*.

Until then I will do nothing, say nothing to divide us. Fà always says she cannot abide a lie, but I think a little discretion is necessary if two lives are to lie alongside each other as quiet as cutlery in the drawer. So I will never let her suspect: my disloyalty to the cause, the weariness that comes over me as I gum down another envelope, the utter indifference with which I set it aside for the post. I will keep my treachery locked up in my heart.

I am making her a cat in alabaster for her fifty-fourth birthday.

Last spring Fà took a solemn vow never to go to bed at night leaving a stone unturned which might help to stop vivisection. My own oath is a more private one. To stand by her in this doomed cause, as in everything else. And with my last breath – because for all her girth and aches, she is sure to outlive me – I will urge her to keep up the good fight. Yes, that's the phrase she will want to hear. I will say it not because I believe, any more, that she or anyone else can save the animals, but because she is most herself in battle. Like the Cavalier in the old poem: she could not love me, loved she not honour more.

Note

My main source for 'The Fox on the Line' is *The Life of Frances Power Cobbe* (1898, 1904); I have also drawn on her *Essays on the Pursuits of Women* (1863) and *The Duties of Women* (1881). A brief mention of the career of Mary Lloyd is found in the Reverend T. Mardy Rees, *Welsh Painters, Engravers, Sculptors* (1912). The poem quoted, 'I have looked coolly on my what and why', is Augusta Webster's 1870 monologue, 'A Castaway'.

After the passing of the watered-down Cruelty to Animals Act of 1876, Cobbe and her Victoria Street Society changed tactics and fought for a total ban on live animal testing (incidentally, a cause yet to be won). After twenty years based in London together, in 1884 Mary and 'Fà' (as Cobbe was called by her intimates) retired to Wales, but continued to be involved in the campaign. When Mary Lloyd died in 1898, her will forbade Cobbe to 'commemorate her by any written record'.

Account

- Games played by James the Fourth, King of Scotland: tennis, bowls, backgammon and dice.
- Year in which the King rode to Drummond Castle: 1496.
- Number of Lairds who had already given their daughters to the King as mistresses: unknown.
- Month in which the King rode to Drummond Castle: April.
- Number of languages spoken by the King: 8. (English, Gallic, Latin, French, German, Flemish, Italian, Spanish.)
- Number of children already born to the King by 1496: unknown.
- Number of hours the King could stay in the saddle without a rest: 10.
- Price of the King's falcon in gold: £150.
- Age of the King in 1496: 23.

- Number of years since the Drummond Clan had locked the Murray Clan into the church at Monzievaird and burnt it down: 4.
- Number of Murrays who died in that church on that occasion: 120.
- Number of Lord Drummond's sons who were executed as a consequence: 1.

- Number of daughters of Lord Drummond: 3. (Margaret, Euphemia, Sibilla.)
- Number of languages in which Lord Drummond's daughters could say 'Yes, Sire': 3.
- Number of Lord Drummond's daughters invited to and installed in Stirling Castle, two months after the King's visit to the Drummonds in 1496: 1. (Margaret.)

- Number of retainers who travelled with the King: 100.
- Time the King's party could spend in each of his castles before the smell from the garderobes made it necessary for them to move on: 3 weeks.
- Number of times a day the King washed his hands: 5.
- Number of new links the King added every year to the rusted chain he wore around his waist as a penance for having let the rebel Lairds kill his father: 1.
- Age of the King at the time of his father's death: 15.
- Number of hands on the King's clock: 1.

- Age of Margaret Tudor in 1496 when her father, the King of England, offered her to the King of Scotland as a bride, and the King of Scotland refused: 7.
- Years in which Scotland and England went to war: 1496, 1497 and 1498.

- Number of daughters borne to the King of Scotland by Margaret Drummond in 1496: 1.
- Number of months after becoming the King's mistress that Margaret Drummond and her infant were sent home to her family: 11.
- Reward received by Margaret Drummond from the King in 1497: a 9-year lease of lands in the earldom of Strathearn.

- Year in which Lord Kennedy gave his daughter Janet to the King as a mistress: 1498.
- Year in which Janet Kennedy bore the King a son: 1499.
- Year in which the King announced that he would in fact marry Margaret Tudor, now ten years old, daughter of the King of England: 1499.
- Year in which the King sent away his mistress, Janet Kennedy: 1499.
- Year in which the King made a formal proxy treaty of marriage with Margaret Tudor, daughter of the King of England: 1502.
- Age of Margaret Tudor in that year: 13.

- Year in which the King took Margaret Drummond as his mistress again: 1502.
- Amount he gave her in gold: £21.
- Amount he gave her for their daughter's nurse: 41 shillings.
- Year in which rumour spread that the King was planning to marry Margaret Drummond instead of Margaret Tudor, daughter of the King of England: 1502.

- Amount the King of Scotland paid an alchemist to discover the Philosopher's Stone: unknown.

- Number of Lord Drummond's daughters who breakfasted together one summer day in 1502: 3. (Margaret, Euphemia, Sibilla.)
- Number of Lord Drummond's daughters who died later the same day: 3. (Margaret, Euphemia, Sibilla.)
- Possible poisoners of this breakfast: 4. (The Murrays; the Kennedys; the King's advisors; salmonella.)
- Number of blue headstones erected in Dunblane Cathedral: 3.

- Year in which the King of Scotland married Margaret Tudor, daughter of the King of England: 1503.
- Annual fee paid by the King of Scotland until 1508 for the saying of masses for the soul of Margaret Drummond: unknown.

Note

'Account' is the story of Margaret Drummond (c.1472–1502), either the youngest or the eldest of the daughters of Lord Drummond, Laird of Cargill, and one of several mistresses of King James IV of Scotland. She and two of her sisters – Lady Euphemia Flemming and Lady Sibilla (or Isabella) Drummond – died after sharing a breakfast in 1502. Family tradition, backed up by very little evidence, claims that Margaret was murdered to prevent her from marrying the King. Their daughter Lady Margaret Stewart was raised in Stirling Castle with the King's other illegitimate children.

Revelations

Friend Mother has drawn all her Children together, more than sixty of them, now, from all over Scotland. She has led them into the sweet fields of Nithsdale, to build their last house.

In her former life in Glasgow her name was Elspeth Buchan – nicknamed Luckie, for her power to survive all trials – but she has cut her ties to the world, and Friend Mother is the only name she will answer to now. She has told her minister, Hugh White, the great secret of the coming times: her Children will not die as other folk will, but be changed, transported into the clouds, to meet with Christ in the clean air and mingle with him forever.

The house the Buchanites have built – called Buchan Ha – is a low barn roofed with heather, with a ladder leading up to a garret where they all sleep on narrow pallets, the men at one end and the women at the other. They have made long deal tables and benches, a meal chest, a dresser, and stools. They have built stout doors with bars, just in case. Already Nithsdale folk are muttering against Buchan Ha, calling it a coop of lousy, fornicating idlers.

Hugh White – the Reverend Minister of the Relief Kirk at Irvine, as he once was – has tried to explain to the neighbours that he and his Brothers and Sisters are not idle but busy. It is already June, in this year that the world calls 1786 but that Friend

45

Mother says is the true Millennium. The Buchanites are busy awaiting the Second Coming.

Only if they renounce the world now, he preaches, will sinful men and women be fit to leave it when the trumpet sounds. Like the disciples who left their nets upon the shore and followed Jesus, the Buchanites have had to resign all earthly drags and entanglements: trades and professions, homes, families even. No one is *sir* or *mistress, husband* or *wife* any longer; there is no more servitude and no more marriage. Only if they live in holy fellowship together, under Friend Mother's close guidance, will they be able to purify themselves for the Coming.

The time is short. The Buchanites have given all their money to Hugh White, to hold and use for the common good. The Brothers work together to dig a well and chop wood, or hire themselves out as labourers in exchange for fresh rabbit meat, bread and turnips; the Sisters share the childminding, washing, mending, knitting, cooking, and brewing of medicines. Everyone wears homespun clothes of light green, which Friend Mother says is the colour of hope.

Hugh is what Friend Mother calls her former minister: one plain syllable. It makes him feel like a boy again. Enemies accuse Luckie Buchan of being mad, or devilish, a ravening old she-wolf that preys on the flock of the true Kirk, but Hugh knows otherwise. He was dust and Friend Mother watered him. He was barren and she made him fruit. When she fixes her eyes on him, he knows he will be with her in heaven, and soon.

One morning Hugh calls the congregation together on the grass outside Buchan Ha, to hear Friend Mother speak.

'What is the body?' she begins, getting out her tinder-box.

'A frail wee house of clay,' says Hugh fervently, 'that will soon cave in.'

46

She nods magisterially. Young James Buchan, one of the three children of her own body, lights her pipe for her; Friend Mother takes a long draw. 'There must be a fast.'

'All day?' asks Hugh's wife Isabel. Of course, Isabel White is not Hugh's wife any more, he reminds himself. Nothing is what it was in the time before.

'For forty days,' Friend Mother corrects her sweetly.

Silence, like quicksand under their feet.

'Like Elijah did,' says Hugh a little hoarsely, 'like Moses. Like Christ himself.'

She gives him a long smile. 'To purify yourselves in preparation for the Coming,' she tells her Children, 'ye must turn your faces against all earthly nourishment for forty days. Not as much as a bannock must pass your lips. Just as a horse is trained for a race, so ye will be strengthened.'

'Strengthened by eating nothing?' asks Isabel White, feebly.

A nod from Friend Mother, who blows out a small cloud of the smoke that helps her preach. 'Just as a goose must be plumped up for Christmas, so ye shall fatten on the Bread of Life.'

No one says no.

The first day is long; they go about their work silently. Everyone goes to bed with an empty stomach. No one is sure whether they are allowed to drink anything, until Friend Mother relieves them by coming round with a pitcher of water with a little molasses melted in it. They gulp it greedily, the adults as well as the children; even Hugh permits himself a cupful. It lifts their mood like wine.

The next morning he wakes flat-bellied, welcoming the new sensation. He feels lighter, purer already; the great hollowing-out has begun.

But in the long garret, six faces are missing: two single men and a family who must have sneaked off in the night to the nearest town. No one says their names. Friend Mother seems satisfied, though; 'This fast will split the sheep from the goats,' she murmurs to Hugh.

Now on her orders the windows are nailed shut and covered, letting in only enough light for reading; this will help them keep the world and the devil at bay. Hugh spends half the second day writing a hymn to inspire the flock. 'Feed,' he repeats under his breath. 'Deed, indeed, decreed, seed, with all speed.'

> *The more on living words we feed,*
> *The less of earthly food we need.*

At sunset the Buchanites go up on to Templand Hill and sing their new hymn. The June air is sweet.

The next day Friend Mother is lighting her pipe when they hear their neighbour farmers outside Buchan Ha, knocking on the heavy planks. 'What heathen goings-on are ye hiding behind barred doors?' roars one man. 'Debauchees!' shouts another, hoarsely.

George Kidd, the former ploughman, climbs to his feet to answer them, but Friend Mother shakes her head and puts her finger to her lips.

'They're bearing false witness against us,' he protests.

'No matter,' she says gently, as if to a child. 'What does it matter what the folk that walk in darkness think of us?'

'But—'

'They'll know their error soon enough, poor souls.'

Strange, thinks Hugh, that no one wanted to come into Buchan Ha until the way was barred against them. That reminds him of something, but he can't remember what. He is a little lightheaded today; distracted by an aching drumbeat in his skull.

48

A violent thump on the back wall makes the Buchanites jump. 'Let us in the house,' comes a deeper voice, 'or we'll burn ye out!'

One of the children starts to cry but Friend Mother smiles placidly, and shakes her head. After a while the abuse dies away; the farmers must have given up and gone home. Hugh sniffs the air for the first whiff of smoke, but there is no fire. He begins to read aloud from the Book of Jeremiah, and Friend Mother goes round with molasses-water, just to moisten everyone's throats for the hymn-singing. They sing higher, and ignore the growling of their bowels.

The first days of the Great Fast go by, and Hugh has never felt so sure of his calling; he knows he must nourish his flock with words. Solid words, sweet words, language tough enough to chew on. No matter how badly his head hurts him, he preaches to his Brothers and Sisters in the morning, at noon and in the evening – the very times when they used to stuff their weak flesh with bread and bacon and small beer. Occasionally a few farmers come by and shout threats or accusations. Once a woman's voice squeals at the window, 'How many bastard infants have ye buried under the floor?' – and Hugh starts laughing, helplessly, and has to cover his mouth with his hand.

At sunset, when the Buchanites can be sure of being alone on their land, he unbars the door and leads them up Templand Hill for a little fresh air. 'I have found out another great secret,' he tells them one evening, his voice high with excitement, and their pale faces lift and catch the last of the western light. 'I have discovered, on reading Scripture, that Friend Mother is spoken of there.'

A hiss of astonishment from the flock.

'I had read it before, but with a man's eyes only,' Hugh berates himself. 'Now I know the truth. Just as evil came into the world through a woman, so it is a woman who must save us. Listen, now, to this passage from the Book of Revelations:

A great portent then appeared in heaven: a woman, robed with the sun, with the moon under her feet and a crown of twelve stars on her head.

See where she comes!'

And he thrusts out his arm to where Friend Mother is walking up Templand Hill in a new gown of yellow stuff, glowing like the last of the sun. She looks as fresh-faced as she ever did before the Great Fast began; he marvels at her beauty, which is not the easy prettiness of youth but a sterner stuff. 'See the stars! Count them!' Hugh urges, running up to her and fingering the twelve places in her loosened hair where black has turned to silver. She submits to his touch, just as the two of them have practised, and then she lifts one warm sole to him as calmly as a mare. 'The final proof,' he roars, putting his finger to it, 'the crescent, the mark of the moon under her right foot!'

The smaller Buchan girl, at the back, lets out a hiccup.

Friend Mother's voice seems deeper today, silkier. 'Grace and peace to you from Him who is and who was and who is coming soon,' she begins.

'Grace and peace,' the congregation murmurs.

'My Children, ye followed me,' she says, stepping up close and looking them in the eyes, each woman and man in turn. 'Ye followed me, leaving your doors open, your washing on the green, your cows unfed at the crib. Ye stood by me two years ago, when the mob smashed our wagons and whipped us into the ditch. Ye let me lead you into the wilderness, followed me all the way to this blessed Nithsdale.' Her voice begins to vibrate. 'Now is coming the time of your reward!'

'What are we to do, Friend Mother?' asks John Gibson eagerly.

'Fast, watch and wait for Christ.'

Hugh can see a sort of flatness in the Buchanites' eyes; they have heard this before. He racks his brains for a way to stir the crowd up.

A girl pipes up now, one of Patrick Hunter's children: 'What does He look like, the Christ?'

Hugh is about to rebuke the girl, but Friend Mother answers. *'His hair is as white as wool,'* she quotes lovingly, *'and his feet are like precious ore as it glows in the furnace. His voice has the sound of many waters, and from his mouth there issues a sharp two-edged sword.'*

Hugh blanches at the image.

Not everyone is strong enough to live on the Bread of Life, it seems. There are murmurings; complaints, even. Isabel White tells Hugh that their children are not well, but he replies that Buchanites are all – old or young – Friend Mother's Children, and she will provide for them.

One morning some of their community – those who joined only a few months before, James Brown and Thomas Bradley among them – force the doors open, saying they will beg scraps at all the farms of Nithsdale rather than hunger like trapped rats in this barn. Hugh and some other strong men try to pull them back inside, but Friend Mother shakes her head and sucks on her pipe. She watches regretfully as the cowards leave, as if they are walking off the edge of a cliff.

The remaining Buchanites have moved beyond work; they spend the days lying curled up on blankets on the floor, listening to Friend Mother's stories. Her words are more vivid than the daylight, more real than the hard ground under their hips. She tells them of the twenty-four thrones and the seven torches of fire, the thunders and lightnings on the glassy sea. Heaven will be shaken like a fig tree and its stars will drop like ripe fruit. The sky will roll up—

'Like a scroll,' murmurs the Hunter girl sleepily.

'That's right, child, like a scroll, and every mountain will be moved.'

The Sisters and Brothers lie still, listening for the first vibration in the packed earth beneath them.

Tonight Hugh cannot sleep, no matter whether he lies on his front or his back or his side. His bladder is full and hurting, but he holds it, because he knows that when he relieves himself it will burn. He gets up at last, fearing that his thrashing about will disturb his Brothers, sleeping only inches apart in the long garret. He steps downstairs softly, and pauses at the door to the tiny storeroom where Friend Mother sleeps alone. He wants to ask something terrible. He is about to say: *how can we be sure this fast is right?*

But as soon as he comes into the room, stooped, dazzled by the light of her wax candle, he forgets his question. Friend Mother is waiting, open-eyed.

She locks him up in her arms.

Afterwards he shudders as if with cold.

'Hugh,' she repeats in his ear, her breath savoury with smoke, 'when I first heard you preach that sermon in Glasgow, my soul swelled with righteous love, and it was clear to me all of a sudden that I must leave my worthless husband and be a witness for heaven.'

He clings on, speechless. He is thinking of his former wife Isabel asleep in the garret above, surrounded by her Sisters.

'But I cannot do this great work alone. I need one man by my side, the chosen one, and d'you know what the name of that man is?'

'Hugh,' he whispers, fearfully.

'Hugh,' she repeats, making a glad chorus of the word. 'Now don't fret.' She stroked his thinning hair. 'You know there can be no adultery, for marriage is no more.'

'Aye.'

'Marriage is a bargain with death and with hell, and such bonds are not to be boasted of or clung to any longer.'

He nods.

'We are partners in the great work. We can do no wrong,' she assures him.

And he tries to believe her.

Friend Mother is fresh-skinned, tireless; the Bread of Life is all the food she needs.

But resentment stirs among the Buchanites. Some have gone missing. And it has been noticed that Hugh goes to Friend Mother's room at night. His wife-as-was speaks bitterly to him in a corner. 'Isabel,' he says sternly, 'look to your own soul, for the time is short.' After that they don't exchange a word.

By the end of a fortnight there is sickness, too, locked up in Buchan Ha. Some are not well enough to walk up Templand Hill at sunset for the hymn-singing. There are cramps, fevers, strange swellings. One of Hugh's children-of-the-body, the boy, vomits up whatever molasses-water Friend Mother gives him. She whispers soothing things in the boy's ear, but he turns his head away. 'They will nevermore hunger or thirst,' she tells him, 'those who are washed clean in the blood of the Lamb.'

Patrick Hunter's daughter appears to be dying; her fever is high, her breath is weak. She has deliriums, sees devils in the ceiling. Friend Mother shakes her head over the girl, and says it is a lack of faith among them that has let this sickness in. Finally she produces a handful of oatmeal from the end of an old sack.

The girl turns her face away in revulsion. 'Friend Mother,' she gasps, 'I need no earthly food.'

'Dear lass, dear good lassie,' says Friend Mother, and gives her another sip of molasses-water instead.

But then Elizabeth Hunter breaks her long silence. She staggers to her feet and says 'We've fasted long enough. June's near over. If Christ was going to come, he'd have done it by now.'

Patrick Hunter belts her with the back of his hand for her blasphemy. The sound silences them all.

Friend Mother comes up close to the woman. For once she is not gentle. 'You value your poor flesh, do you? I tell you this, you besom, the time is very close. If you desert us now, Christ's fire will melt all the flesh from your bones.'

Elizabeth Hunter is clutching her cheek. 'Whatever about myself,' she weeps, 'I'll no watch my daughter and my son and my husband die of famishment before my eyes. Patrick,' she roars at him, 'this is self-murder, so it is, and the murder of your own bairns!'

But he turns his face from her, and so do the boy and girl; when she tries to lift the children in her arms they are dead weights. So Elizabeth Hunter goes off with no companion but Katherine Gardner who used to be her maid in the old days. Katherine begs Andrew Innes to come too, but he spurns her. Hugh watches them go, then turns to count the Buchanites: barely forty of them left. Too few, too few; what kind of welcome party will they make for the Lord?

There is no day or night any more, only this damp, warm, blanketed floor where the remaining Sisters and Brothers lie curled up together like worms. Their breaths are sharp; their faces are sunken. Friend Mother is all sweetness, all patience with their imperfections.

In bed, she interprets the Book of Revelations. 'It has come to me that you are the one called the Great Man Child, my beloved,' she tells Hugh excitedly. 'Is it not written that the woman shall give birth to the Man Child, and the dragon shall seek him out, but he shall be so well hid that the dragon will not find him?'

Hugh smiles up at her, as when he was small and his mother used to tell him stories about bogeys in graveyards. He is drifting, vague, almost asleep. And then he smells bacon.

At first he thinks it is another of the hallucinations of hunger, one of those ghost scents that have been troubling him recently. But no, it really is a bit of lean, purple bacon. She has it in her hand; she touches it to his mouth. He jerks away as if burnt.

Friend Mother is smiling. 'Hugh, don't you recall what the Prophet said? Eat that which is good, and let your soul delight in fatness!'

'The others are starving,' says Hugh hoarsely. He begins to understand. So that's how she still looks so strong, so alive.

'For a little while more, aye,' she says sadly, 'they must be cleansed in preparation for Christ's Coming. But for the leaders there is exemption.'

'Exemption?'

'Yes. You and I must watch over the Brothers and Sisters in their weakness; it is our sacred task. Our strength must not fail, even for one night.' She chews the dried bacon with relish, and reaches under her bed again. Her hand comes up with a whole slice of bread, and she puts it between his lips.

Helpless, Hugh sucks it, chokes it down.

Out in the world it is the month named July, but inside Buchan Ha time has little meaning any more. They live in suspension, in the eternal moment of waiting.

A terrible banging on the door, one morning, and Elizabeth

55

Hunter's voice, shouting 'Open up in the name of the law!'

This goes on for half an hour, with the Buchanites droning their hymns in an effort to drown out the banging on the door, till Friend Mother gives Hugh a weary nod. Being the only one with enough strength left for such tasks, Hugh unbars the door and lets their former Sister in.

She has three constables with her, and a warrant to take her family away. The Buchanites stare at her with their dark-rimmed eyes. Patrick Hunter is enraged by his wife's treachery. 'Bitch,' he spits at her as the constables haul him out into the daylight. The Hunter girl is so weak, she has to be lifted on a rail.

Friend Mother stands by the door, arms folded, watching. 'You think merely of your children's bodies, Elizabeth Hunter,' she remarks. 'I lost some infants myself, back in Glasgow; it pleased God to take them, all but three. At first I complained, much as you do, but now I know their souls flew free.'

At which point, Elizabeth goes for Friend Mother's eyes, shrieking, and has to be pulled off by half a dozen Buchanites. Hugh is deeply moved to see that his Brothers and Sisters can still summon some strength to protect their beloved leader.

She is stern, that night, preaching to the Buchanites where they lie. 'Look into your hearts. If ye be not pure and holy yet,' she tells them, 'ye will be like imperfect clay jars that explode in the furnace.'

The next day the constables come back with another warrant. This time Hugh lets them in at once, to stop the noise of the pounding. They take away two more children, Thomas Bradley and his sister Mary, who is very weak, and raves of goblins as the constables carry her out.

Then Katherine Gardner arrives with an angry knot of Nithsdalers and claims to be with child by Andrew Innes, at which there is a great groaning among the Buchanites. Hugh peers into

56

the young man's face, but cannot decide whether the claim is true or a mere trick. Katherine Gardner demands that they deliver Andrew up to her, lest he die of hunger, and her baby have no father. Friend Mother, blank-faced, inclines her head at last. So the fellow goes off with her and the constables, long-faced, in somebody's jacket that is too small for him.

Hugh suspects Andrew of feeling relieved; rescued. It is a sad fact that weakness lies like a maggot in the heart of most of the Buchanites. Only Hugh loves Friend Mother as she should be loved.

The next day, when the constables bang on the doors of Buchan Ha, it is with a warrant to seek out *any corpses of man or woman or infant who might have been starved or otherwise foully put to death*, but though they search in every dusty corner of the building, they find nothing. Hugh stands with his fingers pressed together like a church. 'See, there is no more death,' he tells them; 'now will ye not believe?'

That night when they are private together in the little room, Friend Mother touches Hugh but he is unmanned, soft as a child. He lies between her legs, his head pillowed on her thigh. The hairs are coarse as mountain grass. This is where he came from, Hugh thinks, dizzy with revelation. All life, all salvation comes out of this cave. A scent drifts up like sharp cheddar, like something baking.

'Take. Eat. This is my body,' she whispers. 'I am the Bread of Life, and he who eats this bread shall live forever.' Her hand on his head. She gives him to feed.

One evening, Friend Mother comes into the long dim hall where the Buchanites lie in a waking sleep, too weak to brush away the flies that occasionally light on their faces. She claps her hands, and the sound is like gunshot. 'Are ye ready?' she cries out. 'Are

57

ye prepared to be translated from flesh to spirit, as a word is translated from a foul gibberish into a holy tongue?'

They are startled, roused from torpor. Hugh stares up at her; she has given him no warning of this.

'Are ye ready for translation?'

'Aye!' they answer in a jagged chorus.

'But the forty days are not over,' says Hugh confusedly.

She throws him an impatient look. 'Christ's days are not measured like ours. I say again, are ye ready?'

'Aye!' goes the general roar.

'If ye are truly ready, Christ will come.'

And suddenly Hugh knows it is true. The spark lights in his chest and flames up. He leads the roar: 'Come, Christ!'

'Soon ye will be eating from the Tree of Paradise,' she tells them, her voice almost singing.

'How soon?'

'Very soon. Watch and wait,' she says, sitting down and lighting her pipe with composure.

Hugh sits at her feet, staring up at her, tense with excitement. 'See,' he whispers to the others, 'Friend Mother's face shines with the glory of Christ.' She is so sure, she is so radiant, how can he ever have doubted?

'Come, now,' Friend Mother says at midnight, clapping her hands again to wake them. 'Time to shed your trinkets. Ye won't need them on the journey.'

There is a clattering like rain as the Buchanites fumble at their watches, rings and lockets, hurling them onto the floor. John Gibson stamps on the crystal face of his grandfather's watch.

'Take your shoes off,' she says now; 'wear your old slippers for lightness, or bare feet would be best.' On an impulse, Hugh runs over to the clothing chest. Time to put on his minister's gown, bands and gloves: his final costume.

At her nod he unbars the door for the last time. They leave it swinging wide. She leads them up Templand Hill by moonlight in their slippers. The countryside is deserted; the green corn stands stiffly in the fields. They go slowly, a caravan of emaciated scarecrows, dragging the weaker Brothers and Sisters, but there is exultation in every face.

They have dragged their stock of wooden pallets with them, on Friend Mother's orders, and now they understand. 'Build me a platform,' she cries out. 'A high platform so I can see Christ's Coming, at sunrise.'

A shriek goes up. *Sunrise*. She has named the hour. At last, at last, thinks Hugh. His cheeks are wet; he finds himself weeping like a boy. The long trial is over.

The Buchanites stack up their pallets crazily, making a rough platform as high as their heads. Hugh waits, then heaves his own pallet on top, for Friend Mother's sacred feet to stand on.

'Bless you,' she says, 'bless ye all,' and takes – of all things – a scissors out of her pocket. 'Drop your hats, your bonnets. All your hair must be cut off,' she instructs, 'except for a tuft on top for the angels to catch ye by, to draw you up.'

'Draw us up into heaven?' asks Hugh's small son, sheltering in Isabel White's skirts, and for a moment Hugh remembers what it was like to love his children – love them greedily, as his own. But there's no more time for that.

'Aye, hen,' Friend Mother tells the boy. 'At sunrise, there will be a light brighter than any light has ever been, and we will all be wafted into the land of bliss; we alone who are worthy, of all the folk that walk the earth!'

She cuts the hair of each man, woman and child. It falls like dandelion seeds around them where they lie on the grass, suddenly weak again, as the night closes in around them. By the last of the moonlight, Hugh watches the transformation. Friend Mother comes to him last; he welcomes the feeling of lightness as the scissors move over his scalp.

Most of them sleep, in the end, but Hugh lies awake beside Friend Mother, his hand in hers, his blood thumping in his veins like a drum. He looks at her but her eyes are closed. He measures the slow creep of the stars.

Towards dawn she wakes, and mounts her platform like a cat, unaided. Hugh thought she might have asked him to share it with her, but really there is only room for one on this precipitous structure, and besides, Christ is coming for all of them; no one will be left behind. Hugh leads his Brothers and Sisters in the chant he has composed in the night. As the first tinge of grey light lifts the sky they clap their hands, they shout it out, panting with excitement.

> *Oh! hasten translation, and come resurrection!*
> *Oh! hasten the coming of Christ in the air!*

Halfway down the hill, a crowd is gathering; Nithsdale men and women, gawking up at the freaks. What matter, Hugh tells himself; no one can hold back the Buchanites now.

> *Oh! hasten translation, and come resurrection!*
> *Oh! hasten the coming of Christ in the air!*

Here it comes, the first yellow ray, sliding over the dark hill.

> *Oh! hasten translation, and come resurrection!*

Their singing mounts to an ecstatic shriek.

> *Oh! hasten the coming of Christ in the air!*

60

Friend Mother is on her feet, her arms out, her hair shining. She has never looked so beautiful. The crop-headed Buchanites all throw up their arms.

Oh! hasten Oh! hasten Oh! hasten translation!

Hugh feels a gust of sweet breeze from the east; surely this is the beginning. Friend Mother dances on tiptoe, as if Christ's arms are around her already; her hair dances. Hugh strains to kick off gravity; under his canonical robes he is hardening, rigid with glory. The breeze scoops the air up, circles, gathers to a blast of wind . . . and the platform, with one long groan, topples down.

Friend Mother is on the ground, on her knees, clutching her left ankle. She rubs it like any ordinary woman. There are smashed pallets scattered around her. Hugh stands still in his shock.

Silence; the chants have all died away. The sun is up, but clouds have slid in from the north, and it looks like a grey day. The Buchanites avoid each other's eyes; some weep into their hands. Below them on the slope, the people of Nithsdale are laughing like crows.

Friend Mother lurches to her feet. 'Christ has been pleased to afflict us with disappointment,' she says hoarsely. 'And do ye know why? Because ye are not yet worthy,' she shrieks, putting out her finger, pointing at each of her followers in turn. 'Ye are lukewarm, unfit for translation. Ye have faltered in faith. Ye have failed me.'

Hugh waits for her gaze to reach him; waits to be singled out as the one follower who has loved Friend Mother truly, who has offered his whole life in her service. He needs to know that he will be with her in heaven. But her eye skims over him as if she does not recognise his face.

She stumbles down the hill. A little later, he follows her.

61

Note

Elspeth 'Luckie' Buchan, née Simpson (*c.* 1738–91), a potter's wife from Glasgow, was one of several women prophets in the late eighteenth century who founded personal cults based on the Book of Revelations. My sources for 'Revelations' include Robbie Burns's letter to James Burness of 3 August 1784; Anon., *The Western Delusion* (1784); Elspeth Buchan and Hugh White, *The Divine Dictionary* (1785) and *Eight Letters* (1785); Joseph Train, *The Buchanites, From First to Last* (1846); and John Cameron, *History of the Buchanite Delusion* (1904).

After the Great Fast, the community was thrown out of Nithsdale by legal means, and settled in Kirkcudbrightshire, where Luckie Buchan died in 1791, promising to rise again in six days, or ten years, or fifty. Hugh White led the remnants of the group to America.

ENJOYED

Revelations
The last rabbits
Ballad
Cued
Dido
Words for things

NOT SO

How a lady dies
Night vision
Salvage
Figures of speech

Night Vision

The other day in the woods I wandered away from the others and kept walking. The ground was soft as porridge. I held one hand out in front of my face and whenever I stubbed my fingers on a tree I felt my way around it. Whenever I stood on an acorn I picked it up for our pigs. I stood still, and there was no sound at all but the wind shuddering in the branches.

I don't think I have ever been alone in my life before, and I am nine years old.

It was Ned and John who found me; I heard them thudding along from a long way off, calling 'Franny! Franny!' Did I not know that I might have caught my foot in a weasel trap, John said, or dashed out my brains against a branch? Ned said our father would have strapped them if I'd come to harm.

My brothers and sisters are mostly good to me. A blind child is a burden, no matter how you look at it.

They're all asleep around me now: John and Ned and Samuel and Dickie in the big bed under the window, Eliza and Mary and Nelly in the one behind the door, and Catherine and Martha and myself in this one, with Billy tucked in at the bottom and Tabby under my arm with her nose digging into my ribs. It's hottest here in the middle of all the arms and legs. The air smells of cheese.

63

When I can't sleep, I make a blank page in my mind, and shapes start filling it. I know about the stars, Father told me. I imagine them flaring through holes in the sky like candles in a draught; the edges must get singed. I wonder about the colour of furze, a bit like strong tea, Father says. (I think colour is when you can taste something with your eyes.) And the mountains around Stranorlar, big as giants blocking the path of the sun. I try to decide how each bird feels to the touch, according to its song. The clinking blackbird would feel like the back of a spoon, but the wood pigeon must be soft as the underbelly of a rabbit.

Our mother is behind the wall, in the kitchen; I can hear her poke the turf. She was so angry, that time I put my hand in the fire, when I was small. But I had to find out what it felt like. She cried while she was wrapping a bit of butter onto the burn. She held her breath so I wouldn't hear her, but I did.

I wish we were all locked up safe for the night. But our father is still at Meeting, and it's all my fault.

Father is Brown the Postmaster. If there's ever a letter for someone living here, it's he who brings it. Most days he sees to the horses that carry letters through Stranorlar and on to all the other villages in Donegal. He lost a toe in the snow once. It's my job to rub his feet by the fire when he comes home. But not tonight.

He walked me to school this morning, as it was my first day. And my last, I suppose. Tonight he's gone to see if the Elders will let him address the Meeting and say how ashamed he is for what his daughter did. I pray they won't cast him out.

I can hear the room filling up with sleep; the little snores, the sighs, the shiftings from side to side. My sisters and brothers hardly know how to move or talk in the dark. They depend on the light so much that once the candle is snuffed out, the greasy air seems to extinguish them too. Night makes no difference to me, except that I can hear better. Tonight I can't remember how to go about falling asleep. My mind bubbles like a spring that cannot be stopped up.

Words have always been my undoing, I can see that now. It began when I was a small child. The sermon was on eternal damnation, and the new Scottish Minister used words I couldn't understand; they echoed in the rafters. So I tried to fix them in my memory, and afterwards, while the brawn was boiling I asked our father to look them up in the dictionary. I never thought there was any harm in it.

Since then I've been collecting words, you might say. They help me to get up, say, when I can't find my fingers on cold mornings. *Fingers*, I say in my head, and there they are, wriggling. Tabby is always bringing me words, even if she doesn't know what they mean. This week I have three new ones: *funereal, ambulatory*, and *slub*. Sometimes for a game, Nelly and Catherine make me say all the longest ones I know; if I won't play, they pinch me. My brothers and sisters think words are to be scattered carelessly, like corn in front of hens. They don't know how much words matter.

Martha, on my left, has curled up like a snail; she has the tail of my nightshirt caught tight between her knees. How can they all sleep so sound when our father is not come home?

What matters even more than words is how they knot on to each other. Sentences are like the ropes the fishermen throw when they're mooring to land. Sometimes they fray, though. Sometimes I put the wrong words in the wrong places, and other times it's not my fault, they'll not fit.

The Schoolmaster says there are rules that govern words, and then there are times when you must break the rules. Mr McGranahan knows everything, or nearly; he knows seventeen times fifty-three. After they come home from school, my brothers

65

say their dictionary and grammar over and over to get them by heart so Mr McGranahan will not have to take down his ashplant. I whisper the phrases while I'm washing potatoes or playing pat-a-cake to make Billy stop crying. Also I have learned Watt's Divine Songs and Gray's Elegy, as well as the Scottish psalms. I made a poem of the Lord's Prayer once, and Tabby wrote it down and said it right back to me. Tabby's only seven, but she's quick at her books. If I had the money I'd feed her till she grew fat as a pig, and send her to a good school so she could come home and read me Greek and Latin.

Some days if there's time after bringing the turf in, Eliza or Mary will read aloud: *Susan Gray*, or *The Negro Servant*, or *The Heart of Midlothian*. I take my sisters' turns at spinning the flax, if they promise to read. I hound them to go on as long as the candle lasts. My ears have learned to swallow up every word; I know a novel by heart after three good listenings. My brothers and sisters think me very clever for this, but it's only a trick for getting by. Like Jemmy Dwyer down at the smithy, who lost his right hand to a horse but can tie knots good as ever with his left.

They are all so peaceful when they are sleeping. I pray to God every night for my brothers and sisters, as I was taught, but sometimes I wish they wouldn't wake up.

Often they all talk at once, like threads tangled in a basket, so I can't hear myself think. The other day while we were spinning, Nelly and Martha quarrelled over whether it is called orange or red when the sun goes down behind the chapel. I know what orange is because we were given one once and I had a piece all to myself; it tasted sharp as needles. Red is the colour of mouths, and of pig's blood, but when it dries it's called black pudding, which is strange. I'm sure I know what turf looks like, from the salty smell of it burning, and milk, from the way it slips down my throat, but they tell me I'm only imagining. Our father tells them, 'Leave Franny be.' He says wishful thinking is a powerful thing, and nearly as good as eyesight.

The other day I told Tabby to open the atlas on my lap, and move my thumb to all the places there are: Belfast, and London, and Geneva, and as far away as St Petersburg. I tried to imagine each place in all its colours. Stranorlar is on the far left of the book, next to the edge; it's a wonder it hasn't fallen off.

There, I'm being fanciful again. Mr McGranahan told me last week, 'You will never go far in life, Miss Franny, if you fall a prey to fancy.' I love the sound of that: a prey to fancy. But I have every intention of bettering myself, and going far in life.

Except that today, I threw away my chance, didn't I?

All might have been well if I could have kept my head down. The Reverend Minister's voice sounded so chilled, this morning, over the scrape he made wiping his feet at the door of the school-house. 'Mr McGranahan,' he began with his Highland r's that go on for ever, 'do not let me interrupt the good work; I merely observe.'

But he butted in after half a minute of grammar, and some-how I knew it was me his eye had alighted on; I could feel his gaze scalding my cheeks.

'Who is that child?' he said.

Now he knew well who I was, for he came to our house on a Visitation not three weeks ago. But the Schoolmaster told him my name, and off they went like dogs in the lane, snapping and scrabbling. The Minister asked the Schoolmaster did he not think it a cruel mockery of such a child to bring her into school. Mr McGranahan said it was I who had begged to come with my brothers, and what harm could it do me?

'Harm, Brother? The harm of making her a laughing stock in the sight of the whole congregation.'

For a moment I was glad I couldn't see; all those eyes turned on me would have been too much to bear.

The preacher went on without stopping for breath. 'To attempt to teach a child so blighted, and a girl at that, is to fly in the face of the Providence that made her so.'

When Mr McGranahan is angry he speaks quieter than ever. 'Nobody gets the chance to teach Frances Brown anything, Brother, so quick is she to teach herself.'

Even then, if I could have kept my mouth shut, he might have saved me. The words behind my lips are no trouble to anybody; it's only when I let them out that I give scandal.

'When I grow up I shall be a poet.'

My words hung on the air like a foul smell. I felt the draught when the boys on either side of me shrank back, as if afraid to catch a fever.

The Schoolmaster began to speak, but my fear made me rush in. 'Mr Milton himself was blind, was he not, Mr McGranahan? Was he not? Did you not tell us so?'

But the Minister was standing over me now, his words falling like hail. 'Milton was a great man. You are a stunted little girl.'

Suddenly I was shouting. 'Does it not say in the Book of Leviticus, *Thou shalt not put a stumbling block before the blind*?'

There was no sound at all for a few moments. I stiffened, ready for the blow that would knock me off the bench. But the Minister only took my wrist between his icy fingers and held my arm up high. When he spoke it wasn't to me, and his voice boomed over my head like the Orange drums on the Glorious Twelfth. 'Who will lead this creature home so she will not fall in the ditch?'

Up close he smelt like vinegar. I ripped my hand out of his grasp. 'I can find my own way,' I said, shoving past the other children, past the long chalky coat of Mr McGranahan, who tried to hold me. I got out the door before I started crying.

As a rule, I can follow any path through Stranorlar and not lose myself, but today I was so bewildered with rage that I very nearly stepped into the ditch opposite the smithy. Only the long grasses at the edge told me I was gone astray. When I got on the right track home I felt the last rays of sun on my face before the mountain snuffed them out.

Once the Browns were great folk hereabouts. Our grandfather's father owned a big stretch of land, but he squandered it all. I can see it in my head if I try: a wet green kingdom, with rivers sliding through the fields like thread through cloth. Now all we have left that is grand is our grandmother's rocking chair. Sometimes our mother lets me sit in it if my feet are clean. Its back is carved with fruit and flowers and shapes that I can't make out no matter how often I trace them with my fingers.

Our mother sits in that chair to do her darning. If I hold my breath now I can hear through the wall the faint creak of its rockers – unless that's more wishful thinking. Our father has been gone for hours. Mother was yawning at supper, but she'll not go in to bed before he comes home from Meeting.

They didn't beat me, when I came home from school, not even when I told them every word I said to the Minister. Maybe they're saving it till tomorrow. I would rather have the beating over with and then I could sleep.

Tabby's face is pressed against my hand on the pillow; I can feel her breath like an oven on my fingers. From the corner, Dickie lets out a faint snore. Martha turns over, without warning, and we all must shift too, myself and Tabby and Catherine and Billy at our feet, all packed together like mackerel in a pot.

If the others were awake I would tell them a story: maybe the one about the cottage that stood in the middle of a village that stood in the middle of a bleak moor in the north country, where lived a certain man and his wife who had three cows, five sheep, and thirteen children. One more than us. Martha likes the tale of the old woman that wove her own hair. Ned prefers the one about the prince with fourteen names.

If I had seven-league shoes and a cloak of invisibility I could be at the Meeting House now. Maybe they're too busy with other matters to discuss a froward child like me. Or else the Elders are arguing with my father this very moment, their big hands thumping the table. But even if I was invisible, it occurs to me, I couldn't make them listen; I couldn't change a thing.

Once when I was small, our mother was teaching me to shell peas. They bounced out through my fingers, and when I reached for them I upset the whole basket. Then I cried, and my mother would have let me go and play on the grass, but my father made me crawl round and pick every pea up off the floor, and then wash the dust off them, for he said he knew I could do whatever I set my mind to. And he was right. But tonight when he was putting on his greatcoat to go to Meeting, he didn't seem so sure.

I bury my face under the blanket and I make up pictures of things that cannot be. A town with seven windmills, and wolves with hair as long as sheep, and a well in the woods that will make anything dipped in it grow. Sometimes in my imaginings I take a wrong turning, and scare myself. Then my thoughts feed on each other like worms in the black ground, but I must bite my thumb and lie still and not disturb the others, because we are so many in one room.

I remember the last three being born. We all heard, through the wall, though we pretended not to. Our mother doesn't make half as much noise as most women, I heard the midwife say. I know I will never make that noise. I am a girl much like other girls, but I'll not grow up to be a woman like other women. Who

70

would have a blind wife if he could help it? But I am a great help with the little ones, our mother says. I've never dropped one yet.

I was just learning to talk when the smallpox got me, so Eliza says. Before that I could see, though I don't remember it. All I have is a sense of what seeing means, and what a colour might feel like.

Some of the Elders told my father that by rights I should not have lived after I was blinded. My father told my mother what was said, and she cried; they didn't know I was listening. And another time when my father asked the Minister the reason for my blindness, he was told it might be a punishment from the Almighty for some sin my parents had committed. But they couldn't think which sin that might have been.

I have a handful of pocks over my eyebrows still; I finger them sometimes, to remind me. The Minister must be wrong. Didn't I live, when bigger children died of the same fever? This must mean that I have been chosen for something. There must be another future for me, if I'm not to be a woman like other women and have twelve children. If I do not grow up to be a poet, then what does it all mean?

A heavy step on the path at last: Father. I hear the tired squeak of the latch. My mother stands up to greet him, and the chair rocks like a branch in high wind.

The voices behind the wall are low, as if telling of a death, but I cannot make out the words. When I sit up, cold air worms its way into the bed; Martha burrows down deeper.

How can I wait till morning?

Tabby wakes when I clamber over her, and mutters something, but I put my hand over her mouth to shush her.

The floor is cold. My nightshirt shifts in the draught as I pull open the door to the kitchen. It makes a terrible creak.

'Franny?' says my mother.

I can smell the fire, and fresh mud on my father's boots. At times like these I wish I could read faces. How can I know what way he is looking at me?

'Here.'

I think he's smiling.

I walk towards his voice with my hand out. Something hard stops my fingertips: a book. I take its weight into my hands and feel its cover; it is not one I know.

'It's called *The Odyssey*. Mr McGranahan says if you bring it in to school tomorrow he'll teach you the first line.'

I turn my face away so as not to wet the paper.

'Go to sleep, now,' says my mother.

Note

'Night Vision' is about the childhood of Frances Brown or Browne (1816–70), known as the Blind Poetess of Donegal, who went on to become a successful novelist in London, living with her younger sister and amanuensis. The best source of information on her is Brenda O'Hanrahan's *Donegal Authors: A Bibliography* (1982). I have also used the autobiographical sketch that prefaces Brown's first collection of poems, *The Star of Attéghei* (1844), as well as her best-known work, the children's fairy-tale collection, *Granny's Wonderful Chair* (1857).

Ballad

After the battle at Philiphaugh on the thirteenth of September in the year 1645, the Army of the Solemn League and Covenant presses north. On the broken road to St Andrews, a cavalryman hangs back till he is out of sight of his comrades, till the dragoons and the musketeers and the regiments of foot have all marched past him. Till the flag, with its stained white cross on a blue field, is gone by. Then he turns off over the empty fields towards Perth. He wears a buff coat with a worn blue ribbon; his hands smell of saltpetre and blood. He is owed four months' wages. He feels nothing, nothing at all.

Bessy Bell an Mary Gray,
They were twa bonny lasses

Scotland is plague-stricken. Folk wear bruises of mauve and orange and yellow for a few days, and then they die. Sometimes, of course, they drop dead before they've had time to bruise. Edinburgh has emptied out like a puking stomach, the cavalryman hears from a passing messenger; the city fathers' carriages are rattling into the countryside. Some say the pest has come down from the Dutch ports on the backs of sailors; others blame an evil miasmus that hangs in the air; others, the war. As he rides along at a leaden trot, the cavalryman thinks of the pest, so he will not have to think of the war. Not the victories; not Marston Moor, last summer, when he was among the Covenanters who helped the Ironsides wrest the whole North from King Charles. Nor the defeats; Kilsyth, a month ago, when the Royalists scattered the Army of the Solemn League and Covenant like chaff on the wind. And in particular he will not think of Philiphaugh, yesterday. There is no end in sight. He will not dwell on it. He will ride on to Perth.

The pest attracts rumours, and the cavalryman hears them all when he stops for water, at various halts on the way. The people say that only men die of it, not women; that it appears as a lump in the armpit, long before the bruises, though others say a lump in the groin; that it is a city sickness, and those who breathe the clean country air are safe; that it is a disease of heat, and if you only last till the weather cools, you'll be healthy all winter. The cavalryman is almost amused to watch how feverishly his countrymen ward off this blight by both science and superstition, washing their doorsteps with lime and wearing their holy bracelets too, nailing up the sick in their cabins for the full of a fortnight so that the taint will not spread. He knows – as every soldier does – that death is whimsical and contrary, and picks whomsoever it chooses, and there is no kind of magic circle a mortal can draw that will keep death out. As he rides along, the cavalryman thinks not of death but of love. Not of one woman but of two.

Bessy Bell an Mary Gray,
They were twa bonny lasses

On the outskirts of Perth stand plague-camps, rough clusters of shanties and tents. In the fields the cavalryman notes the wide square pits, and three shapeless figures with spades, lifting the

74

turf for another burial. He picks up his pace and rides by.

He is stopped at the bridge by a man in an official robe, and asked for a testimonial before he can be let into Perth – a certificate of health, signed by the magistrates of his home town. But the cavalryman leans down off his horse, and says that he has just come from fighting papacy and prelacy and the King's Highlanders, and he wants a bowl of meat and a bed for the night, and he will not be prevented by fiddlefaddlers. And besides, he has no home town but Perth.

At the market there is little left but oats and carrots, but plenty of them, and not rotted. The cavalryman fills his saddlebag. The market woman stands well away from him. She holds out a ladle for his coins, then dips them in a scalding pot of water before letting them into her pocket.

The house on the High Street is locked up. The neighbours say his parents have fled away into the country, but no one knows where. The cavalryman stands staring up at the shutters, scratching a hot bite on his neck, and tries to remember the boy he once was before he ever went to be a mercenary for Gustavus Adolphus in Germany and learned to cut down papists like wheat. The boy who used to sleep behind those shutters, dreaming of fair women. He thinks of Bessy Bell, daughter of the Laird of Kinvaid: his first love, her creamy hair, and her supple neck. And then he lets his thoughts move to Mary Gray, daughter of the Laird of Lynedoch, with her eyes as dark as crow-feathers.

As if he is being led, then, he turns his weary horse towards Lynedoch.

> *Fair Bessie Bell I lo'ed yestreen,*
> *And thocht I ne'er could alter;*
> *But Mary Gray's twa pawkie een*
> *Gar'd a' my fancy falter*

75

Seven miles the cavalryman rides, only seven miles on his stumbling horse, but it is as if he is emerging from a nightmare. There are no plague-camps on this side of Perth; the evening air sweetens as the day cools, and the birds chime in the thick hedgerows. He rides past two labourers at work in a field, and they have their blue bonnets on, and seem as well fed as in the days of peace. His horse startles a plump rabbit from the ditch.

At Lynedoch House he learns that the Laird is gone away on business, and that Miss Gray is holed up in the reed-cutter's hut by the river, for fear of the pest.

One more mile he rides, then, with his head full of what he will say to Mary Gray, and what she may say to him. The last time they met was before Marston Moor, when he was half a life younger. He remembers her red smile, and the sad way she shook her head, when she told him she'd rather walk to John O'Groats barefoot than steal a husband from her friend Bessy Bell. And he told her Bessy Bell was the best of girls, and worthy of such devotion if anyone was, but he was not Bessy's husband nor betrothed, nor had ever asked her, nor would be no woman's but Mary Gray's. At which she shook her dark head at him and went away.

Since then the cavalryman has not caught a glimpse of the daughter of the Laird of Lynedoch, nor written her a letter – for what could he speak of, this last year, but killing? – and not a day has passed without him thinking of Mary Gray. And Bessy Bell, too, if the truth be known, because the two names go together. He has never known such friendship, himself, except briefly in the heat of battle, when you stand back to back with another soldier and know that you would take a bullet meant for him, because that is what soldiers must do. But for such loyalty to last between two girls in the calm light of day – that mystifies him, and draws him all the nearer.

There is the river, a narrow glint in the trees. At first he thinks the reed-cutter's hut is deserted – he can see no smoke – but as he reins in his horse, heart thumping with panic, they come walking up from the water. Two women, not one. Their skirts are hitched up, their pale legs wet to the knees; their arms are laden with rushes. They are laughing, and when they see him they stop for a moment, then laugh even more.

> *Oh, Bessie Bell and Mary Gray,*
> *They were twa bonnie lassies!*
> *They biggit a bower upon the ley,*
> *And theekit it ower wi' rashes.*

There is little need for explanations, in these times. They make him welcome. After the meal – the ladies are grateful for the oats and carrots, having run out of food yesterday, and the servants having failed to bring down any more – the cavalryman helps them mend their roof. Bessy soon gets the knack of weaving rushes into wide patches to cover the holes; Mary, being taller, stands on the table to poke them into place. 'This reminds me of when we were children,' Bessy Bell tells the cavalryman, as easily as if they were old friends and never had been anything less or more. 'Mary and I, we used to make these little bowers, of green branches all carpeted with rushes.'

He stares at her and remembers what he loved about Bessy Bell. Or loves. He cannot tell.

'Hours we spent,' remembers Mary, 'hours and hours squatting inside, playing at keeping house!'

He can picture them so easily, the two lairds' daughters; serious, ceremonial little girls. He wonders what it must be like to have a friend so long that you cannot remember a time before; to be woven together from the root. He is beginning to suspect

77

that no matter what happens in the future – whether Mary Gray ever agrees to be his wife, or not – he will never come between these two. But he feels no resentment, not today.

As twilight falls, the two women spread a sheet on the grassy bank beside the fire, and open their last bottle of French wine. The cavalryman has not tasted such drink in years; his tongue seems to quiver in his mouth. He looks between Bessy's pale head of hair and Mary's black one; between the soft mouth and the scarlet. They talk of a fiddler they all heard once; of the varieties of apples that keep best for the winter; of some thistles in the field beyond, that grow as high as a man. The darkening world shrinks to a fire and its wavering circle of light. Beyond this fragrant, smoky river bank, nothing is real, thinks the cavalryman: no pest, no war, no troubles of any kind. Perhaps this is a game, but it is better than growing up.

> *Young Bessie Bell and Mary Gray,*
> *Ye unco' sair oppress us;*
> *Our fancies jee between ye twa,*
> *Ye are sic bonnie lasses.*

The cavalryman could sit here forever, between the dark head and the blonde, the three of them fixed and firelit like some new constellation in the black night. He has no wish to disrupt this scene by leaping to his feet, taking one woman or another away on his tired horse. All he asks is to stay here by the river, hidden away from the loud and reeking world. All he asks is to be part of this.

And then Mary Gray looks at Bessy Bell, and both of them look at him, and he thinks they are about to tell him to leave them for the night, but what Mary asks is what he hoped she was never going to ask, 'What news of the war?'

He cannot speak. He shrugs.

'Is our Covenant winning? Or is the King?'

This time he cannot even shrug. 'I see no end to it,' he says at last.

'When must you go back to your regiment?' asks Bessy Bell, and in the firelight her eyes shine and he cannot tell why he ever turned from her to her friend; cannot remember when or how that choice was made in his heart, as arbitrary as a leaf's turning yellow or red, as random as a battlefield.

His eyes swim; he is weeping in spite of himself. 'I will not go back.'

They stare at him.

'At Philiphaugh . . .'

'We heard about the victory,' says Mary, smiling at him. 'Were you there, at Philiphaugh?'

He stretches out his fingers, stained red in the glow of the dying embers. 'What it was,' he whispers, 'was not a victory, but a massacre.'

Not a sound from the women.

'Montrose's army had escaped us, but we caught the Irish regiments in a loop. They surrendered in the end, on General Leslie's promise of safe passage to Edinburgh.' He takes a long breath. 'As soon as we had their muskets in a pile, and their officers had ridden ahead under guard, we despatched the men and boys.'

'You mean he lied, the General?'

He can't tell which of the women has spoken. He nods briefly. 'That's war. I've done that much before. But what I must tell you is, what I must say – we were in such a frenzy to avenge our losses at Kilsyth and finish these papist savages for good, we turned on the women.'

A whisper, from one or both. 'What women?'

79

'There are always women, in the baggage train; they follow the camp. How else could the soldiers eat, or wash the lice off their shirts?' He speaks harshly. 'The Irish had their wives with them; three hundred, I'd say, not counting the children. A few dozen were big with child.' His eyes are shut, but he can see it still, in bright colours. 'Our pikemen cut them down, then we troopers moved in with swords. There was one woman – when I sliced her open, the infant inside her fell out on the grass.'

Bessy's arms around him, with no warning. 'Hush,' says Mary beside him, stroking his head like a child's. 'Don't say any more.'

'But—'

'Shhhh,' whispers Bessy and they embrace him between them. They hold his pain and contain it, squeeze it into a tiny ball. There is no more fear, no more horror; there is only comfort.

'Don't think about it,' murmurs Mary; 'it's all behind you now.'

'I won't go back,' he tells them.

'You won't go back. Stay. Stay here with us.'

The cavalryman crouches by the fire, rocked in these women's arms, dazed with happiness. Impossibilities come true. A broken man may be made whole.

'How hot your forehead is,' says Bessy, kissing it softly.

He is drifting, confused. His throat is dry and a little bell rings in his ear. His face is wet with salt water. A fire has started up behind his eyes. He has come so far and now he need never leave. The day was long but now it is time to rest. He blinks up at the stars over the patched roof of the hut.

> They theekit it ower wi' rashes green,
> They theekit ower wi' heather;
> But the pest came from the burrows-town,
> And slew them baith thegither.

He will be dead tomorrow; the women, bruised yellow and orange and mauve, by the end of the week. They will all three lie there on the grassy river bank, like lovers, and the sun will bake them to leather.

Note

'Ballad' was inspired by the macabre song, 'Bessy Bell and Mary Gray'. The lines in italics are quoted from various versions of the ballad, including a nursery rhyme and a comic adaptation by Allan Ramsay. According to a local tradition, recorded in the *Transactions of the Society of the Antiquaries of Scotland* (1781), it was based on the death of two devoted friends, the daughters of the Lairds of Kinvaid and Lynedoch (Lednock) near Perth, who retired to a bower in 1666 to avoid the plague, but were infected by a young man who loved them both and came to bring them food. However, as there was no plague in Scotland in 1666, this anecdote probably dates from the plague of 1645, which decimated the population of Perth.

Come, Gentle Night

A slice of bridescake and a cup of negus apiece and they are off. Effie's parents stand by the front door and wave their hands. John gets in beside her, tucking the lap-rug round her billowing tartan silk skirt. His man Hobbs ropes their trunks on behind, then lifts the collar of his greatcoat and climbs up to ride with the coachman.

A quarter-mile down the road to Scotland the April afternoon begins to darken. John blows his nose with an elephantine roar, leans back and checks his watch. 'Not five o'clock. I'm glad that's over.'

'So am I,' Effie assures him.

'The Reverend Touch's voice is a trifle hoarse for my taste,' he says. 'But considering the necessarily upsetting nature of such solemnities, we all bore up rather well.'

She puts her small hand over his and speaks breathlessly. 'I know you've had a trying fortnight, John.'

'Well,' he says with a sniff. 'Your parents' house is rather chilly.'

'No, but – I've been so distracted about Father's losses on the railroads – he can't do much for us, I know—'

He presses one finger to her lips. 'Not another word of that, my sweet. You're in my hands now.'

'But John, your prospects in life could hardly be called fixed—'

'That's my concern, not yours,' he says with a hint of sharpness.

'But I think your parents mind very much about the settlement. Could that be why they didn't come to the wedding?'

'Nonsense, Effie. I told you, their health didn't allow it, that's all.' In the silence, John gets out his big handkerchief again. His nose is scarlet at the tip, and twitches like a rabbit's. After the carriage has crossed the Tay, and they have caught a glimpse of Scone Palace through the streaked windows, John sits up straighter. 'I can hardly see your face, tucked away in that cane bonnet, Effie.'

'Well, I suppose I might very well take it off, as there's no one to see.' She loosens the strings and lays it in her lap.

'That's much better,' he says, smiling down at her, and takes her hand in both of his. 'Look, such charming heathery knolls,' he exclaims. 'We should see some proper hills in an hour or two. Nothing touches me more than mountainous landscape, nothing in the world,' he says wistfully. 'Not that the Highlands are a patch on the Alps – but time enough for them, when we go to Chamonix with my parents.'

'Will I like Switzerland, John?'

'How could you not?' He gives her a look of kindly exasperation. 'All that remains to be seen is whether you can bear the heat and the fatigue of walking at high altitudes. I do wish I might show you France too, but those wretched revolutionaries have put paid to that plan.'

'Is it true what people are saying,' asks Effie, 'that there could be dreadfulness here in Britain too?'

His eyebrows almost meet. 'Who's been putting such nonsense into your head?'

She speaks with fearful relish. 'A hundred thousand of the Chartists are marching in London today, the vicar told me, and it's said they've gathered five million signatures for their petition, and if they don't get their way there'll be blood shed!'

'In that case, it's just as well we're here in the tranquil Highlands,' he says, grinning at his bride.

After the dark blot of Birnam Wood – where John coughs and blows his nose for some time, in preparation for quoting *Macbeth* – they pass the ruined cathedral of Dunkeld. When the carriage goes over a rock in the road the couple are flung up in the air, and both break into laughter.

'Sorry, miss, sir,' comes a muffled call from the coachman, and Hobbs's upside-down head hangs at the window for a moment, checking his master and new mistress are unhurt.

When the footman's head has disappeared, Effie leans against John confidentially. 'Why did you marry me, I wonder?'

'Fishing for compliments, are we?'

'No,' she cries, stung. 'But you are a brilliant young man of some name in literary and artistic circles, and of all the girls there are in the world—'

'Why did my heart select Miss Euphemia Chalmers Gray, of Bowerswell, near Perth?'

'Your mother once told me,' she remarks carefully, 'that you have a tendency to surround people with imaginary charms.'

'Well, let's consider the matter.' He holds her chin between finger and thumb, at a judicious distance. 'Are Miss Gray's charms of a chimerical nature? *Item*: she has an exceedingly pretty face. *Item*: she is both lively and kind.'

'That's two items in one,' Effie points out, squirming.

'*Item*: she plays Mendelssohn moderately well.'

She makes a moue.

'Now, on the dark side of the scales, to prove my objectivity –'

John growls, '*item*: the same Miss Gray does not always welcome criticism. *Item*: her health is uncertain, and her talents as a walker are so far untried. *Item*: she likes everybody—'

'Isn't that a virtue?'

'—everybody and anybody, which is most definitely a weakness.'

'You're such a queer being!' Effie exclaims with a giggle.

'I?' He makes a face of shock.

'You shrink from society' – she counts on her fingers – 'you write and paint and work like a carthorse, you're prone to dreadful melancholies, and you're besotted with your old Alps.'

'You'll never wean me from them. But I do admit I am an odd fellow,' John says seriously, peering out the window at the encroaching twilight. 'If I had been born into your sex, I doubt I could ever have loved a man like me.'

'Don't say that,' she says worriedly. 'I never meant you weren't easy to love.'

'Well,' says John, rubbing his hands together, 'Heaven never designed men and women to be the same. Marriage is said to be a miraculous yoking of opposites.' He interweaves his cold fingers with hers, till they form a tight roof. 'Whatever may be flawed, or lacking, in each of us, the other will supply.'

They drive on, north by north-east into the ragged hills, and the darkness closes in around them. At Pitlochry, the coachman gets down to light the carriage lamps.

'Tell me, John,' Effie murmurs sleepily, 'how shall we pass our days?'

He pulls at his whiskers, considering the matter. 'Much as we've spent them until now, I hope.'

'Oh,' she says faintly.

'Except of course that we shall be together, in our rented house for the time being. I shall go into London all day, to the British

Museum, or if I'm etching or doing anything that requires good light, I shall go to my old study at my parents' house.'

'Couldn't you do that at home with me?'

'No, no,' he laughs, 'I'd be shockingly under your feet. You'll be busy writing letters to improve your spelling, and trying to read Balzac for your French, and keeping up your piano – though perhaps not for two hours at a time any more, as in your boarding-school days.'

'And I shall have your coat brushed,' Effie murmurs, 'and mend your gloves, and above all, I shall keep you from wearing white hats!'

'And in return, young Miss Gray, you must rein in your extravagant spending—'

Her mouth begins to turn down.

'—and promise never to wear that excessively pink bonnet.'

She sighs like a martyr. 'Pink is my favourite colour.'

'In this instance you must bow to the superior discernment of a man who has made the beauties of Nature and Art his life's study.'

'Very well,' she yawns.

'And also,' he says, pressing his advantage, 'you mustn't let your uncle call you *Phemy* any more. Effie I've named you, and Effie you'll stay. *Phemy* sounds like the kind of restless girl you used to be, who gadded around town to phrenologists and mesmerists and all manner of charlatans!'

Effie ignores this. 'I expect I shall like keeping house, even just a rented one,' she says thoughtfully, 'and before long I shall have – I mean –' and she falters, 'quite apart from any other domestic duties that may arise in the fullness of time.'

She waits, watching his profile in the dim of the carriage, but he does not pick up the subject; he has begun to sniffle, again, and is fumbling for his handkerchief. 'I dare say you will have

86

to call, and be called upon, most days,' he remarks glumly.

'It's not that I'll have to, John; I'll like to.'

'Well, it comes to the same thing.' He blows his nose violently. 'But I trust you won't be flirting with any more young subalterns.'

'John!'

He wags his long finger at her. 'Admit it, Effie, until our engagement was made public, you were a perfect specimen of a man-trap!'

Speechless, she rolls her eyes.

'But no,' he adds more soberly, 'all I really fear is that you will encourage the hordes to pester me.'

'Oh, I never would!'

'You don't seem to understand, my dear, that even now it's only by a firm rudeness that I am able to shield myself against the importunities of acquaintance-seekers, who long to know me, and talk nonsense about art. The social whirl is as much poison to my health as arsenic would be,' he adds fiercely, rubbing at his nose with his damp handkerchief. 'When people try to get at me through you—'

'I won't let them,' she insists, squeezing his wrist. 'Now tell me more about our days,' she murmurs soothingly.

'Well,' says John, lying back against the horsehair upholstery with a wheezy sigh, 'I'll return at four o'clock, shall we say, and present myself in the parlour to take you down to dinner—'

'Papa says I always order a very good dinner.'

'—indeed, and then we shall have delicious hours of quiet tête-à-tête.'

'Oh yes,' she says eagerly. 'You'll show me pictures of beautiful statues, and we'll discuss your book, and your Mr Turner and his wild paintings, and I shall learn to mend your broken pens. But John, will you not miss your bachelor state?'

87

'I should hope not,' he says, smiling down at her. 'You will be a great solace to me; someone to come home to, someone to refresh my spirits and save me from my old despondencies. You'll be my mistress, my friend, my queen, my treasure, my only darling, my own Effie!'

She shudders with pleasure. 'But John,' she says after a moment, tugging at his cuff, 'how do I know you will always love me as you do now?'

He grins at her between nose-blows. 'That depends entirely upon yourself. A good wife has a secret power to make her husband love her more and more every day.' He wipes his streaming eyes and gathers her into his arms. 'And I know this much: God has given you to me, and he gives no imperfect gifts.'

The countryside is a rumpled black blanket, only occasionally lit up by the coachman's swinging lamps. The newlyweds, enclosed in the carriage, cannot see each other's faces any more. At the Bridge of Tilt, Effie lets out an enormous yawn, and murmurs 'That's nineteen times we've crossed water today.'

Past ten o'clock: Blair Atholl at last. Effie is so stiff, Hobbs has to lift her out of the carriage. The inn is almost empty, on this Lenten Monday. Their hostess finds some syrup of violets for John's throat, and brings them some cold beef for a late supper.

Then John and their hostess exchange significant glances, and he stands up and holds out his curved arm to Effie. The newlyweds leave Hobbs downstairs warming his toes at the fire, and follow their hostess's lamp up two flights of creaking stairs. 'This is quite the genteelest room in the house,' she assures them, poking the fire, 'and the rest of the floor is quite empty tonight, so you won't be disturbed.'

Effie studies the drab watercolour of Ben Nevis that hangs over the mantelpiece.

'Might you need any help, dearie?' asks their hostess, nodding at Effie's travelling case. 'Shall I send the maid up?'

The bride shakes her head.

Their hostess sets the lamp down beside the bed with a reverent air, nods to the gentleman, and shuts the door behind her.

When they are alone, John smiles at Effie. 'You must be tired. I confess every joint in my body is aching. Aren't you tired?'

'A little,' she says.

He goes to the window and checks the heavy velvet drapes are quite shut. '*Spread thy close curtain, love-performing night!*' he says rather nasally.

Effie stares at him.

'Juliet's speech after her wedding, don't you remember?'

She nods, smiles tightly. She examines the tall screen, with its enamelled wading birds, then goes behind it to undress.

John's brows draw together as he tries to recall the lines. 'There's another piece about fiery-footed steeds,' he mutters, tugging at the knot of his black silk cravat, 'and something about being sold but not yet enjoyed . . . and then I do believe she says

> Come, gentle night, come, loving black-brow'd night,
> Give me my Romeo; and, when he shall die,
> Take him and cut him out in little stars,
> And he will make the face of heaven so fine
> That all the world will be in love with night
> And pay no worship to the garish sun . . .

He stands in his long nightshirt and cap; a tear glitters in his left eye. Effie emerges in her voluminous nightgown and comes up close to him. 'So beautiful,' he murmurs. 'So beautiful, that image of the stars, and all the sharp little 't's in the third line.'

He reaches out his hand and undoes Effie's plait now, reverently unwinding the three thick loops that encircle her head. She arches her neck like a cat. 'My dear,' he says, halting, 'would you put your veil on again for a moment, as you promised? I barely saw it during the ceremony, in your parents' drawing room; I had my eyes shut almost throughout.'

She laughs a little, and goes to fetch it from her case. 'There,' she says, turning with a flourish.

'Oh, Effie. Oh, my love,' he murmurs, beckoning her to him and pressing his mouth to the fine white lace that lies against her eyelids. 'If I look any longer I may die of joy . . .'

She shivers.

'But what am I thinking of, letting you catch a chill?'

Obedient, she plucks the veil off, folds it away and scurries to the high bed. She has to climb up two mahogany steps. John gives his nose a final wipe and gets in the other side. They stare at each other like children, laughing under their breath. John starts to say something, then hushes, reaches out towards the ribbon at her neck.

But Effie, gathering all her nerve, pulls the nightgown up and over her head in one long rush, and lays herself entirely bare.

A pause, and then John moves close, very slowly, close enough to see her, smell her, drink her in. Effie feels her cheeks scald with shame and pleasure. She squeezes her eyes shut.

Nothing happens. Nothing stirs in the room, and she opens her eyes again.

Something has checked him. His reddened eyes are wary, puzzled.

'What is it, John?' Effie's voice is a squeak. 'What is wrong?'

'Nothing my dear.'

The cold is dimpling her skin, sharpening her nipples now. 'Was I immodest? I only wanted—'

'That's not it.' His Adam's apple moves as he swallows. 'This is such a . . . an unfamiliar situation, would you not say?'

'Oh. Yes.'

'You are . . .'

'What? What am I?'

'So different from the statues.' He produces an uncertain little smile.

'Different,' she repeats. And then, after a long moment, 'In what way, different from the statues?'

He assumes a jovial tone. 'Having all your arms, I suppose I mean, and your head on too!'

She stares at him like a forest creature disturbed on a road.

John gets down from the bed and walks over to the window. The boards creak. The backs of his legs are hairy below the nightshirt. He divides the curtains an inch or two, to look out. 'There appears to be a light on Tulach Hill; perhaps a bonfire,' he remarks softly.

Effie says nothing. She has pulled up the blankets, and wrapped her arms around her nakedness till nothing can be seen but her white face, her spilling hair.

He turns at last, decisive. 'My dearest,' he says, sitting on the edge of the bed and crossing his legs, 'what do you know about the relations of married people?'

She stares at him. 'Their parents, you mean? And brothers and sisters?'

'No, no—' and he smiles a little twistedly. 'I'm referring to . . . marital relations. Has your mother explained anything to you of such matters, by any chance?'

She shakes her head, looks down at the counterpane.

'What few ideas you have on the subject must come entirely from literature, then.'

'I suppose so,' she mutters, her cheeks dark with embarrassment.

91

'What worries me,' says John thoughtfully, 'is that you may not realise the risks entailed.'

'Risks?'

'Marital life, in this special sense, is not to be entered on lightly. You are so very young – not yet twenty – and your system has been subjected to such anxiety about your father's monetary troubles – and it occurs to me now that the gentlemanly thing to do might be to postpone the whole business.'

'Postpone it?' she repeats. 'But I wouldn't mind – I mean, I am prepared to take any risks that, that need be taken—'

He interrupts, tapping the counterpane. 'Also, I dread that any ill-health on your part might disrupt our expedition to the Alps with my parents. The double excitement of travel and marital relations could prove too much for you, Effie, as it often has for women of stronger constitutions. And then if there were to be any immediate consequence—'

She blinks at him.

'A child, I mean,' he says gently, 'why, we might not get to cross the sea again for ten years!'

Her mouth turns down at the edges; her crimson lip is trembling.

'Believe me, my sweet, if I am willing to control myself, it is for your own good.'

'Yes,' she says through her teeth. 'But John—'

'Oh, my love,' he interrupts, 'I am asking you to trust me to decide this, as your husband. But of course, if at any time in the future your views depart from my own – if you at any point find that you wish consummation to occur without further delay, for the sake of your own health or happiness – all you have to do is tell me.'

'Tell you that I wish it?'

'Yes. Truly, Effie. For instance, I would do it this very

night if I felt it was your wish,' he says eagerly. 'Is it?'

'No,' she says, looking away to the edge of the candlelight, 'no, of course not, John.'

He grins at her. 'I think you're somewhat relieved, isn't that so?'

'Perhaps,' she whispers.

'The more I think about it, Effie, the more I see that our marriage should be based on the soundest spiritual principles, not mere passion.' His voice rises in enthusiasm, as if he is lecturing on art; his cold seems to be gone. 'And in the fullness of time, my dear, when I make you my wife in that special sense, I think we will both be glad that we showed forbearance tonight.'

'Perhaps so.'

'It's a bargain, then. Our little secret bargain.' John holds out his hand, and she puts hers into it, and he presses his hot mouth to the backs of her fingers.

Then he picks up her discarded nightgown as easily as a nurse, holds it high so that Effie can slip her arms in. He plants a kiss on her pale forehead. 'Sleep in my arms, now, my darling.'

She edges down into the blankets, into his heavy embrace.

'You'll need all your strength for tomorrow's early start, and the long drive to Aberfeldy. Goodnight, my love.'

'Goodnight,' she whispers.

But after the candle is out, he and she both lie awake in the smoky darkness.

Note

'Come, Gentle Night' is about the wedding night of Euphemia 'Effie' Chalmers Gray (1828–97) and the art critic John Ruskin (1819–90). They met in 1840, when she was only twelve, and were married eight years later at her parents' house at Bowerswell, near Perth, on 10 April 1848. My sources for this story are family letters and legal documents included and discussed in Mary Lutyens' books *Effie in Venice* (1965), *Millais and the Ruskins* (1967), and *The Ruskins and the Grays* (1972), as well as other biographies of Ruskin.

In 1854 Effie ran away from her husband and had their marriage annulled on the grounds of non-consummation. A year later she married the painter John Everett Millais, with whom she had eight children.

Salvage

The Cottage Ladies were breakfasting when word came.

Cousin Anna slid into her self-propelling chair and got as far as the front door.

'Wait!' cried Cousin Sarah. She took hold of the padded handles of the chair and bumped Anna carefully down the steps. On the path, Anna wheeled herself along with frantic thrusts of her hands. Sarah had to jog to keep up with her cousin; she lifted her skirt in both hands. The rain was over, but the October wind cut at Sarah's ankles and neck like a willow switch; she wished she'd thought to bring her Kashmir shawl.

When they reached the beach, the damp brown sand clogged the great wheels of Anna's chair, and she slowed to a grinding crawl. Sarah caught up with her, then, and started pulling the chair along backwards. Anna stared over her shoulder across the half-mile of pale Norfolk strand, across the dark splintered waters, to the ship. The two of them breathed in gasps. They didn't need to say a word.

The main mast was down, Sarah saw; the old red brig was keeling over sideways, as if drunk, or poisoned. On its side was a word in strange, angular letters. The wreck held to the invisible rocks under the hard grey water. Small oil-skinned figures could be seen here and there, roped to the rails. As the ladies came to a standstill and watched, a wave reared up foaming and bit the deck.

'Poor souls,' said Sarah, but the wind ate up her words.

Her cousin's eyes were narrowed against the spray, like chisel marks in her wide Nordic face. 'You there!' Anna cried, pushing a strand of rogue hair back into her cap. 'Ned Sylvester!'

One fisherman left the little knot of men and ran over, hands folded respectfully. 'Miss Anna. Miss Sarah,' he added, with a sideways nod. 'She's a Ruskie, seems like.'

'Never mind where the ship's from. Why aren't you using the Apparatus?'

Sarah looked past the fishermen and there it was on a hand-barrow, the Patent Life Saving Apparatus, on which she and Anna had spent half their savings. According to the advertisement in *The Times*, it could shoot a rope across the sea twice a minute with the greatest degree of precision. But its iron curves bore traces of salty rust already.

'She's too far out for that,' said Ned Sylvester, wiping his nose on his sleeve. 'No hope for much but salvage this time, we all reckon.'

'Don't say that.' Anna's cheeks bore two red marks.

'Well, Miss,' said Sylvester uncomfortably, his eyes shifting back to the shore.

'Have you so much as tried the thing yet?'

He shook his head, not looking at her.

'Come along, then.' Anna jerked her head at her cousin to wheel her down the wet sand to where the other fishermen stood staring out at the wreck. 'Exert yourselves, men!' she shouted. 'Send for the Life Boat, and set up the Apparatus.'

Sarah stood beside one of the fishermen's wives. She realised she was shivering; the wind off the sea was colder than she'd realised. 'Has word been sent to Mr Fowell Buxton up at the

96

Hall?' she asked at last. Her voice was too faint; she had to repeat the question.

The woman nodded, never taking her eyes off the listing ship.

Sarah watched her cousin, who was directing half a dozen fishermen to fire off the Apparatus. Anyone would think their forebears — Anna's and hers — had been naval heroes, not Quaker wool merchants. How well this particular spirit would have hounded Bonaparte's fleet, Sarah thought, if it hadn't had the ill-luck to be lodged in the body of a crippled female.

She'd mentioned that one evening, while they were toasting muffins at the fire. But Anna would have none of it. 'What earthly use are *what ifs*?' she'd asked, pulling a golden muffin off her long fork and reaching for the honey. 'I was born in the body allotted to me. Of course, if I hadn't been dropped on the stairs at two months, I might have been an elegant dancer today at twenty-seven years old.' Her mouth curled up to show Sarah how little that vision impressed her. 'But I get by. I may be a crip-pled old hulk, but I get enough breeze to fill my sail. I can swim and shoot as well as Cousin Fowell, can't I?'

Sarah nodded obediently.

'I can wheel myself to our carriage and go to Meeting' — Anna counted these feats on her fingers — 'I can grub around in the literatures of several ancient nations, I can mount petitions on behalf of the emancipation of the slaves, and someday, Sarah' — she threatened her cousin with the blackened fork — 'someday before we die, you and I will journey to the Tyrrhenian Sea.'

Sarah had smiled back at her, foolishly glad.

But today what faced them was not the Tyrrhenian but the English Channel, a steely monster that was clawing the foreign ship to bits. Sarah heard a muffled bang from the Apparatus now, and the first rocket went off; the thin woven-hide line snaked out of the basket as the mortar carried its tail high in the sky like a

97

kite. The powder left an after-scorch on the chilly air. Another bang followed, then another – like fireworks on Midsummer Eve, except without the splashes of coloured light. Some of the foreign seamen were waving, Sarah saw; one was at the rail, locked on with one elbow, straining to grab the flying rope so he could make it fast and pull himself in to shore, hand over hand. She felt his panic in her bowels, and had to look away for fear of letting out a moan. She squinted into the grey howling morning, but couldn't see where the mortars had landed. 'Did it work?' she called to her cousin.

No answer: evidently not. The men were reeling the mortars back in now, like leaden fish. Anna was almost at the water's edge, her wheels deep in the scored sand, her frantic arms over her head, signalling orders. The wordless fishermen put their backs to the Apparatus and ploughed it right down to where the waves covered their boots. Ah yes, Sarah saw it now with a thrill, that would get the ropes ten yards closer to the seamen. Not much of a distance, except that it might mean life rather than death. Another flash, and this time Sarah could see a mortar soar across the sea maybe three hundred yards – but fall just short of the ship. Twenty-four pounds of iron, dropping like a clay pigeon.

This time when the men hauled the ropes in, two of the lines came all in a rush; their mortars were missing. Ned Sylvester examined one frayed end; Miss Anna waved her finger in his face like a desperate schoolmistress. 'I told you to soak the ropes at Easter, didn't I? Didn't I warn you they'd break if they were allowed to dry out?'

It seemed to Sarah now that there was an awful slowness to everything, because there was nothing left to do. The little soaked figures on the deck had stopped moving. They were no longer individuals, about to catch the lifeline thrown to them, but a body of strangers watching for their death in every wave.

Next time she looked away from the ship, she saw Anna's chair stranded in half a foot of water, the rim of her skirt dark with water. 'What were you thinking?' Sarah scolded her cousin, hauling her back up the beach.

'I was thinking of the seamen,' said Anna shortly, her eyes locked on to the ship. 'Thousands of souls choke to death on salt water on British shores every year, and all for lack of equipment and readiness.'

'I know,' said Sarah, her throat sore.

The men were in a little huddle over the Apparatus. Anna squinted up the beach. 'They told me the Boat had been sent for, but where is it?' She let out a harsh sigh, and pushed her shoulders back. 'We can't expect much of the poor. It's up to people of property to organise matters and set an example of courage. Those who can, I mean,' she added bitterly.

Sarah stared at Anna, whose forehead wore its old badge of pain: three lines across, one down. 'Cousin,' she said, halting. 'My dear. You've saved many lives.'

'Vicariously,' came the answer, very crisp.

'What difference—'

'The difference is this,' said Anna, twisting round in her chair to face Sarah, 'that in my library I can act for myself but here on the shore, when lives hang in the balance, I'm shackled to this chair, as feeble as an infant. As trapped as a rabbit in its hutch. Besides,' she added, cutting Sarah off, 'I've saved no one today, have I?'

Their eyes turned back to the ship. A gigantic wave smacked it from behind and there was a terrible groaning of old wood.

'She's breaking up,' said Anna through her teeth.

'No,' said Sarah, but only because she couldn't bear it, not because she didn't believe it. After a minute, she added, 'I sometimes wonder . . .'

'What?'

She spoke with some diffidence. 'What sort of God lets these things happen.'

'These things, meaning wrecks?' asked Anna harshly.

'Yes,' said Sarah, 'and other things,' her eyes on her cousin's motionless knees, skinny as a dog's under their blanket.

Anna kept staring out at the splintering ship. 'The same God who made the seas for us to sail on,' she said finally.

'But—'

'We can't have it both ways,' snapped her cousin. 'Either we're free, or we're safe; take your pick.'

But Sarah hadn't picked, it occurred to her now. There had never been a moment where her life had forked like a pair of paths in front of her. She'd come to the Cottage as a child to do lessons with her Cousin Anna, and she'd never left, that was all; she'd been content to let her life happen to her, like weather. Perhaps she lacked a sailing spirit.

A yelp went up now from one of the fishermen, and turning, Sarah saw Fowell come loping down the beach. His servants behind him toiled to drag the little wooden Life Boat.

'Cousin Fowell, at last!' called Anna.

He was breathless, red-faced; his neckerchief hung dishevelled on his broad chest. He opened his mouth to speak to the ladies, but there was a terrible ripping in the air, and they all stood and stared as the foreign ship broke apart. Tiny figures slid, disappeared into the dark cave in the waters. Sarah thought it almost obscene to watch, but couldn't turn away. She seemed to feel the water in her own lungs.

'All lost,' wheezed Fowell.

But Anna pointed mutely.

'What?' asked Sarah.

'There,' said Anna, 'among the wreckage. I'm sure I saw a head.'

Sarah looked at her cousin's red-edged eyes and pitied her as she was never usually allowed to pity her; pitied her more than she pitied the drowning seamen, though she couldn't have said why.

'My dear—' began Fowell kindly.

Anna let out a scream. 'There! Two of them, holding to the mast!'

And then for a second they could all see the foreigners, the two dark, minute heads, the bodies dragging along behind the broken mast as it heaved and dropped on the waves.

'The tide is washing them this way. Get the Life Boat into the water.'

'It's too rough, Anna,' Fowell told her. 'The men won't risk it.'

'Poltroons! I'd go in myself if I had the strength.'

At that he turned his back, as if offended, but he was heading for the Life Boat, Sarah saw; he was beckoning to the servants to drag it down to the slashing edge of the waves. The wreckage had drifted in another twenty yards on the tide. Sarah's mouth was dry with excitement.

After a brief discussion the ladies couldn't hear, Ned Sylvester got into the Boat with Fowell Buxton and hauled on the oars, face wide in a grimace as he fought the incoming tide. As soon as they pulled away from the sand, the Boat was tossed and spun about like sea scum.

'Still a good ten yards between them and the sailors,' muttered Anna.

Sarah rested her hand on her cousin's bony shoulder, delicately, and Anna took hold of it with cold fingers, and held tight.

The waves blocked the ladies' view; one moment it looked as if the Boat was almost upon the wrecked mast to which the two sailors clung, the next, as if the whole ocean had rushed between

101

them. Sarah wanted to pray, to ask for these men's lives as a favour, but she knew that was sheer superstition. All she could do was wait on the Spirit.

'Ned's throwing a rope,' yelped Anna. 'One of the sailors has hold of it . . . yes, they're hauling him in!'

The seaman looked like a waterlogged bag of grain as Fowell Buxton pulled him from the sea. The ladies watched the little Boat swing and dip under its new weight. 'And the other?' Sarah peered into the salty wind.

'They've thrown him the line,' said Anna. 'It's no more than two yards away. What's wrong with the man?'

Despair, thought Sarah suddenly. All he had to cling to was this splintered mast. What could persuade him to let go of it? Why should he believe a skinny rope would save him?

'Cousin Fowell's kicking off his boots,' Anna reported in a chilled voice.

'What?' Sarah stared, wiped her eyes to clear them.

'He's going in.'

'No,' said Sarah. 'Not at his age. Surely he wouldn't dream—'

But Anna was already halfway down the beach, her wheels grinding through the sand. 'No. Cousin, no!'

The men in the Boat gave no sign of hearing her shrieks. Fowell Buxton stood up in the wavering Boat for a moment, then dived over the side. The first wave ate him up.

'No!' Anna shrieked again, though she must have known he couldn't hear her.

Sarah was by her side. 'He's a strong swimmer. I'm sure he's got a rope around his waist. The water's not too cold for October . . .'

Anna's teeth were bared to the wind. 'It's my fault. I called him a poltroon.'

There was nothing to be said. All they could do was watch

102

for Fowell's greying head between the blades of the waves.

He emerged at last where they weren't expecting him, on the other side of the mast. His soaked head was barely recognisable, more like a seal's than a man's. He was struggling to break the seaman's armlock on the wreckage. It looked more like a murder than a rescue. Anna muttered something Sarah couldn't hear. A gigantic grey wave came up and covered everything.

It could have been a matter of years, rather than minutes, later, when the ladies glimpsed Ned Sylvester leaning from the Boat to pull the two men in. Sarah kept counting heads, unable to believe.

The Boat's keel made a musical scraping on the shore. As the fishermen's wives surrounded the seamen to lift them out in blankets, Fowell Buxton staggered up the beach. 'Ladies,' he said, as if a little drunk, at a ball. Brine poured from his sleeves, and there was a twist of bladderwrack in his hair.

'Cousin Fowell,' said Anna, with a hint of amusement.

Sarah wrapped him in her arms, not minding the wet. She started to cry.

'Now now, no need for that, my girl,' he said. 'Come, Cousin Anna, we've need of your tongue. Surely among all your twenty-odd languages there'll be one these poor foreigners understand.'

She rolled her eyes at his exaggeration, but wheeled herself directly towards the huddled group around the seamen. One of the foreigners was being sick on the sand, retching up salt water. Anna addressed herself to the other, who was looking round him in a dazed way. After a few minutes, she called back to her cousins. 'Good day,' she said, almost laughing. 'He says good day, or perhaps that it is a good day; I can't be sure.'

Fowell was drying his head on a towel that one of the women had brought him. He cleared his throat with a wet roar now and

103

wrapped a blanket round his shoulders. 'Lift them into that barrow,' he ordered, 'and have them come up to the Hall. There's plenty of room in the barn and I'll send for someone from Cromer to nurse them.'

But as the two men were being wheeled up the beach, the more alert one wailed in protest and climbed out of the barrow. Anna caught up with him as he was crawling down the beach; she bent out of her chair to touch his wet head.

'What is it now?' asked Fowell, his nose streaming. He looked at Sarah and raised his eyebrows. She gave a little bewildered shrug.

'Wait,' Anna told them. Then, after another exchange of strange guttural phrases, she said over her shoulder, 'As far as I can tell – though the dialect is a strange one – they want to save themselves.'

'Save themselves?' shouted Fowell. His nose was purple. 'Save themselves from what? Why would we have bloody well saved them from drowning if we meant them any harm?'

Anna went into another huddle with the sailors, then straightened up in her chair. 'I have it now. How stupid of me. The word must correspond to *salvage*. It appears they want to stay to see what can be saved. From the water, you know.'

Fowell let out his breath in a baffled puff. 'Nonsense. What's there to salvage that's worth their catching their death?'

Sarah stared out at the gnawed, splintered remains of the Russian ship. She wondered what detritus the tide might bring in, tonight or tomorrow. A barrel of spirits? An odd shoe? A scattering of wet letters from home? The bodies of their lost shipmates?

But Anna wheeled herself past Fowell up the beach to Sarah. Her face was marked with the wind's radiance. 'Let them be. Come along,' she said. 'We'll fetch them more blankets and flasks of hot wine.'

Sarah tucked her numb hands in her armpits, turned and followed the snaking tracks of the wheels up the sand.

Note

Anna Gurney (1795–1857) and her cousin Sarah Buxton lived in Northrepps Cottage, near Cromer on the Norfolk coast, and their neighbours called them the Cottage Ladies. As well as being a linguist and historian who published the first modern English translation of the *Anglo-Saxon Chronicle* in 1821, Anna was known for her attempts to rescue drowning sailors.

My main source for 'Salvage' was G. N. Garmonsway's invaluable piece of research, 'Anna Gurney: Learned Saxonist' (in *Essays and Studies*, 1955), which draws on unpublished letters and family anecdotes. I also consulted the anonymous *On the Means of Assistance in Cases of Shipwreck* (1825), which has been attributed to Anna Gurney.

Anna Gurney and Sarah Buxton acted as their relative Fowell Buxton's secretaries in his long campaign to end the slave trade, founded a school, travelled to Rome and Athens, and were finally buried together in the seaside graveyard at Overstrand.

Cured

P.F., aet. 21, single; admitted into the London Surgical Home Jan. 7, 1861

'My brother brought me in. He's a peeler, I mean a policeman.'

'Do you keep house for him, Miss F.?' The doctor crossed his legs, and his wing chair gave a luxurious creak.

The walls of his office glowed with books. The carpet was thick under her scuffed boots; she wanted to sink down onto it and sleep. The pain kept her always tired, these days. 'Yes, well, no. I used to be a cook with a very good family, you see, Doctor Brown.'

He smiled at her a little reprovingly. 'Mr.'

'Oh that's right, you said, pardon me. I mean Mr Baker Brown, sir.' The doctor's face was smooth-shaven: no whiskers, even. He had the pink glow of a best-quality pork sausage, she thought, and almost laughed at the thought. Then she remembered the question. 'When my back got so bad, I could hardly stay on with that family, could I? So my young brother, he's always been good to me – our parents have gone to their reward so there's only us now – my brother said he'd take me in till I was well again.'

'But you have not been well for a long time now, I believe?' Mr Baker Brown's eyes were tender, respectful.

'No, sir,' she said, letting out her breath and feeling that familiar throb start up again in the small of her back. 'I've been to the free hospitals and they can't do a thing for me. One doctor said I, what was it he said, according to him he said I showed no signs of organic disease, only the normal aches and pains of life!' Her voice was getting slightly shrill, so she covered her mouth with her hand.

Mr Baker Brown tutted faintly.

'So in the end, not that he can afford it very easy, but my brother has some savings put aside, and he said he'd pay for me to come to this special new clinic for female health, seeing as you're said to be the *ne plus ultra*.' Whatever that meant. The borrowed phrase felt foolish in her mouth. 'My brother knows nothing of medicine, of course, sir, but he knows what he's heard; one of the sergeants at the station has an uncle that has a wife that came to you with a weakness of the chest last year, sir. He – the uncle, I mean – says he knows nothing about your methods except that they work, and his wife is a changed woman!' She was aware she was talking too much; she couldn't seem to stop. 'And in the waiting room' – she jerked her head over her shoulder, and felt the familiar twinge – 'I heard one lady tell another that you're the wisest man in Christendom when it comes to women's sufferings.'

Baker Brown smiled with wry modesty. 'To speak frankly, Miss F., I see myself – being both a doctor and a gentleman – as a protector of womankind.'

'Like the knights in the old tales?' she asked, fascinated.

A little nod. 'It appears that destiny has called me to rescue the softer sex from the general ignorance of their friends and advisors. I am a pioneer, so to speak, in a wholly new branch of the healing sciences, but I must do myself the justice to admit that my efforts have already met with a considerable amount of success.'

'So my brother heard,' she murmured, her eyes tracing the gold-backed spines that filled the nearest bookcase.

'Well,' said Mr Baker Brown decisively, 'together we must ensure that his generosity is well repaid.'

'Together?' Miss F. spoke a little hoarsely.

'Indeed.' He uncrossed his legs and leaned forward, all at once, with his hands joined. She heard the slippery leather of his chair squeak. 'For the truth of the matter is that I can only cure a patient who truly wishes to get well.'

Her breath was released like a flame. 'Oh I do, I do indeed, sir.'

He gave her his hand. 'I could tell that about you, Miss F., the moment you were shown into this office.'

She got to her feet slowly, her lips pursed against the sudden pain.

There will be wasting of the face and muscles generally; the skin sometimes dry and harsh, at other times cold and clammy. The pupil will be sometimes firmly contracted, but generally much dilated. There will be quivering of the eyelids, and an inability to look one straight in the face.

The examining room was painted in dazzling white. The nurse had taken her behind a screen and changed her street costume for a loose white nightgown. Now she lay on a padded leather table and stared into the bright eye of the lamp.

When the doctor came in his manner was brisker and more animated. He carried a notebook and a fountain pen. 'Where exactly is the pain at this moment, Miss F.?'

'I don't know that I can rightly say, sir. About at the middle of my back, perhaps? It's not so very bad when I'm lying flat like this, you see, just a stiffness and a heaviness, really, but dreadful when I walk or try to lift anything.'

'And also when you rise from a chair, I have observed.'

'That's right,' she said, suddenly grateful to the point of tears. 'That's when it pierces right through me, like a sword. At least, that's what I imagine, though I've never gone into battle.' She gave a nervous little laugh.

'Mercifully not, Miss F. Brave as woman may be in the age of Victoria, she is still exempt from that particular patriotic duty!'

As he said that he took her by the wrist. Miss F. looked at the wall. She couldn't remember this ever happening to her before, except with a friend of her brother's, at a party, once, who'd taken her hand when everyone was admiring the tableau of *Britannia's Subjects Pay Her Tribute*. Mr Baker Brown was left-handed, she noticed, but not at all awkward. He pressed her wrist a little harder, and stared down at the fob he held in his other hand. She felt thrilled, comforted.

'Your pulse is regular,' he murmured, 'but a little quick for my liking.'

'I've always been sturdy, till two years back,' she assured him. 'I can tell you exactly when the damage was done: I was sugaring caraway seeds for Christmas, on the mistress's orders, and the boy was nowhere to be found, so I had to lift the heavy kettle of syrup off the fire myself, and I felt something rip in my back. I said it to her the minute she came in, the lady I worked for I mean, but she said it was nonsense as backs can't rip.'

Mr Baker Brown was jotting something in his notebook. 'Until I've examined you fully, I cannot make any firm pronouncements,' he murmured, 'but I can tell you now, Miss F.' – his warm eyes suddenly rose to meet hers – 'that it is generally impossible for the non-medical to penetrate into the root of their condition.'

'Oh.'

'The incident you describe may have revealed your disease, rather than caused it.'

109

'I see,' she said again, and blinked up at him. 'I was sure that was it, the sugar syrup, I mean, sir. My brother said I didn't ought to work for a lady who'd treat me that way.'

'Your brother's natural concern for you' – and here the doctor flashed her another of his smiles – 'leads him to fancy that he can form an opinion on medical matters. Are you ever constipated, Miss F.?'

'Yes, at times, I suppose,' she said, startled.

'Does it hurt to defecate, at those times?'

'I . . . I suppose so.' As Baker Brown began to press lightly on her stomach, she turned her face to the wall again.

'Any pain, now?'

'No, sir.'

He touched her face, and she flinched. 'Skin moist and warm,' he commented under his breath, as he wrote it down, and she smiled a little, though she couldn't have said why.

Then he leaned down and Miss F. thought for a moment that he had lost his mind, that he meant to kiss her. She went stiff from head to toe. 'Breath inoffensive,' the doctor murmured, straightening up, 'and now if you would be so good as to let me see your tongue.'

She put it out, but only a little; she couldn't stick out her tongue at a gentleman. He felt the tip of it, put his index finger in her mouth and pressed down, fingered her gums all over. Her eyes swam; she blinked hard. No one had ever touched her that way before, inside her mouth. She kept her tongue very still, and memorised the smooth cool surface of the doctor's finger.

His eyes seemed to narrow a little now, as her brother's did sometimes when he spoke of gathering clues, tracking down a thief. 'Do you suffer from giddiness, Miss F.?'

'Occasionally, on first getting up, in the mornings,' she said.

'Headache?'

'If the day is hot. When I was a cook I did; my cap was too tight.'

'Do you perspire freely?'

'Sometimes,' she admitted, looking away. That was a nasty question.

'And your menstrual periods, are they irregular?'

She felt the blush flood up from her collarbones. 'I don't know,' she faltered. 'Maybe. Sometimes.'

'Do you suffer from them at more or less the same point in each month?'

'More or less.'

'Is the flow excessive?'

Excessive, she repeated in her head. What was the definition of excess? 'Sometimes.'

'Do they last as many as four days?'

'Five or six, usually,' she confessed.

Mr Baker Brown shook his head as if that was a bad sign. Then he went to the end of the table. He put his warm hands on her ankles and pressed them apart.

She clamped her knees together.

'I beg your pardon, Miss F., and I respect your delicacy, but this is necessary for me to complete my examination.'

She squeezed her eyes shut and let him part her legs. She started counting from one to a hundred, but she only got to eleven. She wondered why he was standing there peering down at her, and what he was looking for. She thought perhaps it was almost over, and then he touched her somewhere. It was not a part she had a name for, or not one that could be said aloud. She writhed a little. She told herself she need not be embarrassed; this was no ordinary man but a doctor, no ordinary doctor but the famous Mr Baker Brown who understood women as no other man in the world did. She thought of stuffing rabbits with forcemeat and rosemary. She lay there; she shook as if with cold. His hands moved like a pickpocket's, gliding, seeking.

Finally he shut her legs, wiped his hands, and helped her to ease herself up into a sitting position. Her back ached. She smoothed the nightgown over her knees, observing the creases.

'Miss F., do you ever suffer from maniacal fits?' he asked thoughtfully, letting go of her arm.

'No, sir,' she said, startled.

'Have you any other symptoms you care to mention to me?' He fixed her with an intense look now, though she couldn't tell why.

She gave him what she hoped was a brave smile and straightened a little, where she sat on the edge of the leather table. 'No, Mr Baker Brown. Really, my back is all that troubles me,' she said, laying her hand quite high up, on the left. 'The pain generally begins just here—'

'Have you any, ah, pernicious habits?' It was the first time he had hesitated in asking a question.

'No, God forbid,' she said. 'Except for a sup of fortified wine. At Christmas,' she added hastily.

A flash of what looked like irritation crossed Mr Baker Brown's pink forehead. 'What I meant to ask, Miss F., is whether you have ever in your life touched yourself? In an improper way, I mean?'

She stared at him.

'In a way that only a physician should touch you, or a husband, if you had a husband?'

Her cheeks were scorching. 'I don't . . . I don't know what you mean, Doctor. I mean, sir.'

'Never mind,' he said lightly, and glanced at his notes again. She had the feeling he was not pleased with her answer. 'Would

112

you say that you feel languid, debilitated? Not so lively as when you were younger?'

'I suppose so. Because of my back.' She spoke mechanically. Her heart was still thudding.

'Can you compose your mind sufficiently to write a letter?' he asked.

'Oh, I would,' she told him, relaxing a little, 'if I only had the time. When I'm not resting I have to see to my brother's dinner, and his collars and cuffs, and I'm slow because of my back, as I said. The pain comes on so sudden—'

'Are you ever sleepless,' he broke in, 'or do you wake in the middle of the night?

'Only if my back is bad,' she said, aware that she was repeating herself.

'Unaccountable fits of depression?'

'Well. Not really.' She tried to think. 'Only a sort of lost feeling, once in a while, when I consider my future.'

'Attacks of melancholy without any tangible reason?' he said encouragingly.

After a moment, she shook her head. 'If I'm ever low in spirits, sir, it's for a reason.'

He put something down in his notebook. She wished she could have a look at it. She thought perhaps if she could tell this doctor all her reasons, all the real and unreal worries that ever lowered her spirits, she would then be able to shake them off. If this gentleman with the broad shoulders under the smooth black jacket were to write down all her troubles, she might stand up in the end, pain-free, released.

The patient becomes restless and excited, or melancholy and retiring; listless and indifferent to the social influences of domestic life.

113

Baker Brown snapped the notebook shut and screwed the lid onto his pen. 'Miss F.,' he began in the voice of one announcing good news, 'forget your back.'

She looked at him and trembled with shock. Forget her back? After two years of nagging, stabbing pain? After two years of being accused of malingering? 'Don't you believe me, neither?' she asked, forgetting her grammar.

'Of course I do. Your pain is real,' he said, bending towards her, and his eyes were earnest. 'But what you are suffering from is a profound disease that affects your whole body and mind, not just your back. You are a victim of a loss of nerve power.'

'Nerve power?' She repeated the unfamiliar phrase.

'It is brought on by peripheral irritation. It is all too common among women of every position in life.'

'But – but why?'

Mr Baker Brown shook his head sympathetically. 'You know from your own experience that the female body is an exquisitely sensitive mechanism. This loss of nerve power, this hysteria—'

She flinched from the word.

He put his warm hand over hers. 'I don't use the word in the layman's sense of female delusions. Hysteria is all too real a disease. You are a respectable young woman who has fallen victim to a terrible, but curable disease.'

'Curable?' she repeated.

'Yes, indeed. By means of a revolutionary new treatment which I first pioneered in this very clinic two years ago. Recently I treated a working woman like yourself, a dressmaker from Yorkshire who had been so ill with paralysis of the arms as to render her unable to do any work for five years.'

'And what happened?' asked Miss F, knowing the answer.

His face shone like a preacher's. 'Two months after she entered this clinic she left it, restored to health.'

114

'No.'

'She has never had a day's illness since,' he said, marking off each syllable with his finger.

Her head was whirling. Could it be true? 'And, and what is this miraculous treatment?'

Mr Baker Brown smiled, almost shyly. 'My dear Miss F., I doubt your education – though clearly not negligible – has been such that you would understand the technical terms.'

'Of course not,' she said, mortified.

'But what I can assure you is that under my personal care you will soon become a happy and useful member of society, and the sister your brother deserves.'

'You can cure me?' she asked, like a child needing to hear it again and again.

'Trust me,' he said softly.

Often a great disposition for novelties is exhibited, the patient desiring to escape from home. She will be fanciful in her food, sometimes express even a distaste for it, and apparently (as her friends will say) live upon nothing.

She didn't want any dinner; that first afternoon; all she asked for was a cup of tea. It was bliss to lie in this snowy white bed and be exempt from all responsibilities. She fancied her back felt a little better already. She had a moment's guilt when she thought of what all this was costing her brother, and another when she wondered who would wash his collars and cuffs for next week, but then she put all that out of her mind. As Matron kept saying, 'What you need is quiet.'

There was a curtain hanging round her bed; it reduced her world to a pure rectangle. Behind her curtain, several paces away behind their own curtains, lay other women, she knew, but she

115

had no idea of their names; Matron called them all *Miss* or *Ma'am*. In the next room was someone Matron spoke of to a nurse as *her Ladyship*; imagine that!

Mr Baker Brown advised against conversation between the patients, according to Matron; when they gossiped they only increased each other's anxieties.

Quiet, that's what Miss F. needed, what all the intricate bones and muscles of her back needed, what her whole body and mind had needed for years. *Nerve power*; she thought of it, bubbling up in her like hot punch. Was this absolute rest the treatment, she wondered; was the miracle as simple as that? Her empty stomach gurgled; she felt light as air.

Later, the lights were extinguished. In the fragrant dark, Miss F. rolled over on to her front, to ease her stiffness. She was tired, but not sleepy. The hard mattress pressed against her chin, her ribs, her knees. She thought of that strange thing the doctor had said about touching herself, the question he had put to her after the examination. She thought of the examination. She moved, but only a little, back and forth against the mattress, as if rocking herself to sleep; so infinitesimally that someone looking in through a gap in the curtain would have noticed nothing. She thought of the doctor's hands.

Mr Baker Brown visited Miss F. twice, on the first morning she woke up in the ward, and twice again on the second day. He asked her about her memories of when she was a girl, and wrote down all her answers. She had never felt so interesting.

On the third day Matron woke her very early for a warm bath.

'Is this part of the treatment?' Miss F. asked eagerly, rubbing the small of her back to loosen the night's stiffness.

A brief nod from Matron. 'It clears the portal circulation.'

'What's that?'

'Nothing you need worry about.'

116

Miss F. lay back in the enormous bath and let the water ease her aching spine.

Afterwards Matron helped her on to a trolley and wheeled her through the corridors. The wheels squealed. In her torpid state, Miss F. heard voices leak from rooms as she rolled past them. She thought she was being moved to another ward, one closer to Mr Baker Brown's own office, perhaps, so he could keep an eye on her state of health himself from hour to hour. Perhaps he would lay his hands on her back to feel if the healing had begun. She had no objection. She had no objection to anything.

There he was, the doctor himself, broad and magnificent in his black jacket. He was pouring something onto a pad of gauze; perhaps some kind of ointment. Miss F. smiled up at him from the trolley.

'Are we ready?' he asked her, and she opened her mouth to answer, to tell him that she had always been ready, that she had been waiting for him her whole life. He brought the pad down over her nose.

The patient having been placed completely under the influence of chloroform, the clitoris is freely excised either by scissors or knife – I always prefer the scissors.

In her dream, she was walking up the aisle on her brother's arm. Mr Baker Brown stood facing the altar, looking straight ahead, but she could tell by the set of his shoulders that it was her he was waiting for. She turned to smile at her brother but found that he'd put on his policeman's uniform, for some reason, and he was angry with the doctor, and he was pulling his long leather truncheon out of its loop. She tried to get between the two men. She felt the truncheon come down and smash her head into pieces.

In her dream, she woke and went to lift the vast kettle of syrup

117

off the fire. As she set it down she lost her balance and slipped in head first. Through the burning she could taste the sweetness. Her screams made no sound.

In her dream, she woke and found herself walking through London to her old house, where she was cook, because she knew she'd lost something. She'd left it behind her, whatever it was; she must have tucked it under her mattress or hidden it under a floorboard. But when at last she got to the right house, instead of going up and knocking on the door, she found herself walking right past. Her legs wouldn't take her up the steps. They wouldn't take her where she needed to go. She looked down and she had no legs, no body at all; she was a ghost.

This time she really did wake. Someone held a tube to her lips, and she sucked, and it was cool water.

'What?' croaked Miss F. at last. 'What's happened to me?'

'You've been in a delirium,' said Matron professionally. 'It's the opium. It's usual, after an operation.'

'What operation?'

'You'll be all right now.'

The time required for recovery must depend, not only, as has already been hinted, on the duration of illness, but also on the peculiar temperament of the patient.

Miss F. was kept in a small private room, far from the others. There was a nurse hemming sheets beside her bed, every minute of the day.

'Why won't you answer my questions?' she begged.

'I'm not here to tell you nothing, Miss,' repeated the nurse. 'I'm only here to make sure you don't touch that bandage again.'

'I just wanted to see. I don't know what's happened to me. I never bled like that before in my life.'

118

'That's because you touched the bandage,' said the nurse.

Miss F. was prescribed bread in milk, strict quiet, and no visits. She had olive oil rubbed into her chest, for strengthening. When she tried to look under the bandage again, her hands were pulled back and tied to the bed. She couldn't stop weeping. 'Something must have gone wrong.'

'It couldn't have done,' said Matron sternly. 'Mr Baker Brown is a most celebrated surgeon throughout the Empire.'

'Then what has he done to me?'

No answer.

'Why won't he see me?'

One morning Miss F. woke up alone. The bandage had been taken off and her hands were untied. She did touch herself then, slowly and deliberately, for the first time. She learned her new shape. There was no pain, down there. There was nothing at all.

The next morning when she woke from her drugged sleep, Mr Baker Brown was there. She thought at first he was only another hallucination. She lay looking up at him, his smooth, unworried forehead. Then she flung herself at him.

But her nails must have been cut short while she was asleep, she realised, because she didn't manage to leave so much as a scratch on his face, only a slight pink mark under one eye. As if the doctor had brushed against some rouged lady at a ball.

She lay flat, feeling a tide of pain surge up and down her spine. He held her hands flat against the mattress – gently, as if she were a child – and called in Matron to tie them down again.

'Why have you mutilated me?' Miss F. howled.

'I have done nothing of the sort,' said the doctor. His eyes were full of hurt. 'I have performed an operation to prevent you from harming yourself, from making yourself gravely ill to the point of epilepsy, lunacy and death.'

She stared at him, her eyes throbbing.

119

'An operation, I might add, which has earned me the admiration of my peers, and material success, as well as the gratitude of countless women and their families.'

'I want my brother,' she said.

The strictest quiet must be enjoined, and the attention of relatives, if possible, avoided, so that the moral influence of medical attendant and nurse may be uninterruptedly maintained.

For six days she was quite alone. She lay on her pillows as limp as an old dress. Sometimes she lay on her side, either the right or the left, it didn't matter. On the seventh day, Mr Baker Brown came in to look at her again. 'My dear Miss F., you strike me as rather better. Your skin, your circulation – Matron reports an improvement in your digestion—'

'My back hurts,' she said, her eyes following him around the tiny room. 'My back hurts as much as it ever did.'

He shook his head at her, almost playfully. 'You sleep well these nights; you eat,' he coaxed her. 'Why won't you admit to being a little better?'

'Because I'm not,' she said through her teeth. 'I demand to be let go. I want to go home to my brother's house.'

'Come now, Miss F., you must know that's impossible. Matron has told you, I never discharge a patient till she is fully cured. Not just cured in body, but in mind.'

Her eyes locked on to his.

'Why don't you do a little knitting?' he suggested. 'Or try to walk to the window and back?'

She cleared her throat. 'How can you bear what you do?'

He spoke with a forced calm. 'Miss F., I must tell you frankly that I believe I have rendered you more truly feminine – more

120

healthy in your natural instincts – more prepared to discover real happiness in marital intercourse, if marriage is to be your lot in life, and why should it not, now?'

He meant every word he said, she could see that in his burning eyes. That was the worst thing, that was the pity of it, it struck her now: that he believed absolutely in his mission. 'I'm going to tell my brother what you've done to me,' she said levelly.

A cautious look came over Mr Baker Brown now. 'I think not. These are delicate matters,' he advised her. 'I have found, in other cases, that the relatives and friends of my patients do not care to pry into the details of treatment, either before or after.'

'When my brother hears my back is no better, after all he's spent—'

The doctor spread his hands. 'He understood from the start that I could make no guarantees about any particular symptom.'

She lay watching him. 'The minute you let me see him, I'll tell him just what you've done to me.'

'I very much doubt that,' said Baker Brown mildly.

She stared.

'For a woman of your pretensions to modesty and respectability, Miss F., to attempt to convey such intimate information to a young man – her own brother – who would be mortified, I imagine – who would cover his ears at such shamelessness in a sister, or run out of the room – what words would you use to make your complaint, may I ask?' He waited.

'I would tell him—' she growled at last.

'Yes?'

She imagined the conversation; her brother's face. All the words that came into her head appalled her. 'I would tell him . . . that part of me has been damaged. Stolen. He could have you charged with assault!'

'I'm afraid he would not understand which "part" you mean.

He is not a man of much education.' A pause. 'How would you describe the "part" to him, Miss F.?' Another moment went by. 'Would you point, perhaps?'

She tried to gather her spit but her mouth was too dry.

'My dear girl, we really mustn't quarrel,' said the doctor, sitting on the edge of her bed. 'At this early stage of convalescence, such confusion, such delusions of having been harmed are not uncommon among my patients. But let me assure you that every note I have written down over the years, every piece of evidence I have gathered with the full force of scientific rigour, proves that my operation works.' His voice was evangelical again; there were tiny beads of sweat along his hairline. 'I swear to you, Miss F., I have seen women who were morally degraded, monsters of sensuality – until my operation transformed them. Women have come to this clinic in a state of desperation, complaining of pain in one organ or limb or another, or even in rage, talking of divorces, and afterwards I send them home restored, to take up their rightful places by their husbands' sides. There are many countries in the Empire, Miss F., where a primitive form of my operation is done on every girl at the age of puberty, to ward off the disease of self-irritation before it has a chance to take hold! Why, some might say—'

This time she did manage to spit.

Mr Baker Brown took out a white handkerchief and wiped his chin. 'The day will come when you will get down on your knees to thank me,' he said shakily.

She looked at this man, into whose hands she had entrusted herself, and knew all at once that he was not the beloved saviour she had been looking for, nor an omnipotent demon either – only a man. A middle-aged man.

A month is generally required for perfect healing of the wound, at the end of which time it is difficult for the uninformed, or non-medical, to discover any trace of an operation.

Three weeks after the surgery, Miss F. got out of bed. She stood straight, testing her balance, shouldering the old pain. Her back felt much the same but she was changed, in more than one way. She knew what she had to do.

'I understand from Matron that you feel quite well today?' Mr Baker Brown asked, marching in.

'Yes, sir,' she said levelly.

'Have you lost all your old symptoms?'

'I have.'

'How are you sleeping?'

'Well.'

'How is your appetite?'

'Well.'

'How are your spirits?'

'Well.'

He looked up from his notebook. 'Your manner is still not a cheerful one.'

'It never was.'

He checked his notes again. 'Can you defecate without the slightest uneasiness?'

'I can.'

She waited till he had finished writing. She knew it was over. 'And Doctor? Sir?' she added, stony-faced.

He glanced up, his eyes wary.

'I'm cured of all my delusions.'

He stared back at her. He blinked once, twice. 'Matron,' he called, 'bring in Miss F.'s street clothes.'

Jan. 31. Discharged from the Home, cured.

123

Note

'Cured' is based on Isaac Baker Brown's brief notes on the case of 'P.F.' in his *On the Curability of Certain Forms of Insanity, Epilepsy, Catalepsy, and Hysteria in Females* (1866), and all passages in italics are from that controversial bestseller. Famous as one of the most skilful surgeons in England, Baker Brown (1812–73) began performing clitoridectomies on women, and on girls as young as ten years old, in 1859. His enemies accused him of destroying women's reputations and leaving them frigid by performing a pointless operation without the full knowledge of patients or their families.

In 1867, as a result of publishing his book, Baker Brown was expelled from the Obstetrical Society and had to resign from his private clinic, the London Home for Surgical Diseases of Women. I have drawn on Ornella Mosucci's excellent essay, 'Clitoridectomy, Circumcision, and the Politics of Sexual Pleasure in Mid-Victorian Britain', in *Sexualities in Victorian Britain*, ed. by Andrew H. Miller and James Eli Adams (1996).

Clitoridectomy never became very well established in British medical practice, soon being replaced by the more fashionable ovariotomy operation – which again had been pioneered by Baker Brown in the 1850s. But in America, clitoridectomy was widely performed until the early twentieth century. (These days, about two thousand female babies a year in the USA undergo surgery to correct 'clitorimegaly', which means being born with a clitoris that a doctor thinks looks too big.)

Figures of Speech

I Mary Stuart O'Donnell Countess Tyrconnell, daughter of Rory the O'Donnell, niece of Red Hugh the O'Neill, bearing the name Stuart as a gift of his Gracious Majesty King James, being of sound mind on this fourteenth day of June Anno Domini 1632 at my villa near Genoa do hereby make my last will and testament.

The Countess is the shape of a cathedral. Under the dome of her belly lives a prisoner who took sanctuary last winter but now hammers to be let out. The Countess's cheeks are porcelain, glazed and cracked with sweat in the light that slants through the olive trees.

Bell comes out with a bowl of cherries.

'How's the child?' asks the Countess.

'Sleeping,' says the lady-in-waiting. 'How goes the work?'

The Countess tosses down her quill. She turns the paper over and presses it down, letting the ink stain the little table. 'What use is it to make a will,' she asks vindictively, 'when everything belongs to my damnable husband, who's off whoring his way round Genoa?'

Bell shrugs elegantly. 'You should write a history, then.'

'A history of what?'

'Yourself.'

A snort from the Countess. 'That's been done. Don't you remember the Spaniard's book?'

'It was full of lies.'

'Ah, but they last longer than the truth, as fruit is better preserved in wine than water.' She bites a cherry. 'Besides, I've run out of time for storytelling.'

'You're only twenty-five!'

'This one means to kill me.'

'Nonsense, my lady,' says Bell sharply. 'You bore your first as easy as a peasant.'

'But this time my whole body says *wrong, wrong*.'

'Aren't the Irish famous breeders? We're as known for it as rabbits! You'll live to drop a dozen children or more.'

The Countess hoists her brocade skirts to her knees. 'Look at these legs, Bell, swollen up like marrows.'

'It's the heat.'

'The heat doesn't make ordinary women faint twice a day.'

'Since when have you been an ordinary woman?'

The Countess smiles grudgingly, spits a cherry stone onto the grass.

'Shall I read to you?' asks the lady-in-waiting, taking a seat.

'Perhaps.'

'Dante? Tasso? The poems of Madame Labé?'

'No. I'm too restless.' The Countess arches her back against the hard wood of the chair. The obscene bulge of her skirt catches the sun. It is as if she is swollen up with memories that will give her no rest until she releases them.

'You should write your family's story, if you won't write your own. That would make a stirring tale.' Bell's voice is only faintly mocking. 'Who has not heard of the O'Donnell and the O'Neill, the glorious Flight of the Earls?'

126

'Ha! When I was a child, no one ever told me that was just a figure of speech.' To distract herself from the twinge under her ribs, the Countess bites into another cherry; it carries the faintest hint of rot.

'You mean—'

'Yes, I pictured them, my father and my uncle, hand in black-haired chieftain's hand, you know, soaring across the Irish Sea like cannon balls.'

Bell lets out a yelp of laughter.

'And really, when you look it in the face,' says the Countess, 'it was an inglorious business, their so-called Flight. My uncle at least could be said to have been a great lord. But what did my father Rory ever do but rule Ireland for a matter of months in his brother's wake, then scuttle away to the Continent with a hundred men and his baby son?'

'Sometimes courage means knowing when to run,' observes Bell.

'Well he might have risked arrest for my poor mother, at least! Couldn't he have kept his ship waiting a single night for a wife laden down in the saddle, great with child? Had he no curiosity to see my face? He couldn't have known I was only going to be a daughter.'

Bell shrugs again, more sympathetically.

'What I used to dream of at night was even more stirring,' says the Countess reflectively. 'The Return of the Earls! My father and my uncle, coming back for my sake. What ships they would have mustered, what guns they would have carried, what glories would have returned to Ireland if that pair of drunkards hadn't died of Roman fever in their first year of exile.'

'Instead, you grew up like a good traitor's daughter, and followed in their footsteps,' Bell points out.

'It was hardly the same.'

127

'Wasn't it an adventure, though, my lady?'

'Our days of youth, you mean?'

'Sneaking round Hampton Court behind the English King's back, hearing Mass in secret, hatching mad plots of escape—'

'Mad they may have been,' says the Countess, 'but what choice had I? How could my grandmother ever have thought it?'

'What, that you'd marry a Protestant at her say-so?'

'That I'd drop the Holy Cross like some limp-wristed ninny, yes,' says the Countess severely.

'Well, since you put it that way.' Bell is amused. 'Your grandmother was no match for you. Though, to give him his due, it was John who hatched the plan of putting us in breeches.'

The Countess's face falls at the name. 'We never should have leagued with that fellow,' she says coldly.

'He was your cousin, after all. The blood of the O'Donnell's.'

'He was a bastard, with no right to claim the name.'

'Come now, the man did get us away from Hampton Court with our heads still on. It was that or the Tower,' argues Bell. 'Do you remember picking our disguise names?'

'We sat up half the night at it,' remembers the Countess, then her eyes flicker as if she is in pain.

'Rodolphe, and Jacques, and Richard,' says Bell, like a litany. 'We wanted to sound like three ordinary young bucks, setting sail for the Continent.'

'No, I wanted to go back to Ireland.' Mary Stuart O'Donnell's voice is mutinous.

'Ah, but the winds turned our ship from west to east, three times,' Bell reminds her. 'You can't argue with your fate.'

'Don't tell me what I can't do,' snaps the Countess. She squeezes her eyes shut.

'What is it?' asks Bell, serious. 'Have the pangs begun?'

The Countess nods once. She picks up a pair of cherries, but

128

cannot eat them; she tosses them to a passing crow. 'Some days,' she says slowly, 'I would gladly trade every ancient marble, every purple hill, every jug of wine in Italy to be back in the County of Kildare.'

'I like this place, myself,' says Bell, gazing at the olive trees.

'At Poulaphouca waterfall there was a sprite, you know, that took the shape of a horse if you looked into the torrent for long enough. In the castle where I grew up, you had to keep one eye out behind you for the Wizard Earl, who was said to have dabbled in magic until he turned himself into a blackbird. On windy nights you could hear him pounding by on a white horse shod with silver. My nurse promised me that when the horse's shoes wore down, the Wizard Earl would come back and free Ireland from English rule.'

'Did you picture him as your father?'

'Of course.' The pain girds the Countess now; she holds her breath until it lets her go.

'Do you remember, on our flight from England, when the three of us were caught in that storm in the Alps, and your moustache was washed away?' Even-voiced, Bell is trying to distract her mistress. 'And that ostler that called you *hermaphrodito*!'

But the Countess is frowning. 'To come all that way, through Flanders and France and Italy, lauded as an Amazon and a Martyr for the Faith – to be received by the Pope, like my father before me – and end up nothing but John's wife!'

'On the road,' Bell reminisces, 'you used to warn him, if he got me a great belly you'd put your gun to his head and make him marry me!'

The Countess laughs all at once till tears stand out in her eyes. 'Somehow I never imagined it would happen to me. I thought I was above the lot of womanhood.' She doubles over, now. 'Holy Anne be with me, this creature has claws!'

129

'Oh, I bought you this from a pedlar,' says Bell, pulling what looks like a twig out of her pocket. 'It's a bit of Saint Anne's own kneebone, the best thing for a birth.'

'Shouldn't I rely on the Sacred Name of Jesus?' quibbles the Countess, panting.

Bell shakes her head. 'Only the Saint cares to ease women's pain.'

The Countess grabs the bit of bone, encloses it in her fist.

Bell scans the horizon in the direction of Genoa. 'John might be home by nightfall.'

'And sparrows might plough fields,' spits his wife. 'That man's going to end up drinking himself to death, in the best O'Donnell tradition, before his children are old enough to know his face. And what I cannot reconcile myself to,' she says, talking fast and breathing hard, 'is that after all my exceptional adventures, I, a hero's daughter, am going to die like any ordinary woman, in a bed of sweat and blood and *shit*.'

'You won't die,' said Bell sternly.

'No?'

'Not this time. I know these things.'

'Liar.' The Countess smiles through gritted teeth.

'Then after your confinement you can invite that Gentileschi woman from Naples to paint the pair of us.'

'As Judith with her maid; that's her speciality.'

'Knives dripping blood!'

'Oh, Bell.' The Countess stops laughing. She clutches her skirts. The waters have come down, seeping through her petticoats like the Po when it mounts its banks.

'Come in, now, my lady,' says Bell. 'It's time.'

'What about the cherries?' gasps the Countess, distracted.

'Leave them for the birds.' She takes her mistress by the sweating hand and leads her in.

130

Note

'Figures of Speech' was inspired by the *Dictionary of National Biography* entry on Mary Stuart O'Donnell, Countess Tyrconnel (1607–49) by Richard Bagwell, which mentions an unhappy letter she wrote to Cardinal Barberini, in February 1632 when she was pregnant for the second time. A heavily fictionalised Spanish biography of the Countess's early adventures was published by Albert Enriquez in Brussels in 1627; my main source is the French translation by Pierre de Cadenet, published in Paris in 1628 as *Résolution courageuse et lovable, de la comtesse de Tirconel, Irlandoise*.

Nothing further is known of Mary Stuart O'Donnell, except that she survived this second childbirth and lived another seventeen years.

Words for Things

The day before the governess came was even longer. Over a dish of cooling tea, Margaret watched her mother. Not the eyes, but the stiff powdery sweep of hair. She answered two questions – on the progress of her cross-stitch, and a French proverb – but missed the final one, on the origin of the word 'October'. Swallowing the tea noiselessly, Margaret allowed her eyes to unlatch the window, creep across the lawn. She thought she could smell another thatch singeing.

The next morning woke her breathless; one rib burned under the weight of whalebone. The dark was lifting reluctantly, an inch of wall at a time. Practised at distracting herself, Margaret reached down with one hand. She scrabbled under the mattress edge for the buckled volume. But it was gone, as if absorbed into the feathers. Confiscated on her mother's orders, no doubt. Clamping her eyes shut, Margaret focused on the rib, bending her anger into a manageable line. She lay flat until the room was full of faint light that snagged on the shapes of two small girls in the next bed.

Her belly rumbled. Margaret was hungry for words. None on the walls, except an edifying motto in cross-stitch hung over the ewer. Curling patterns on the curtains could sometimes be suggested into letters and then acrobatic words, but by now the light was too honest. She shut her eyes again, and called up a grey, wavering page with an ornate printer's mark at the top. 'The History of the Primdingle Family,' she spelled out, 'Part the Fifth.' Once she worked her way into the flow, she no longer needed to imagine the letters into existence one by one; the lines formed themselves, neat and crisp and believable. Her eyes flickered under their lids, scattering punctuation.

The black trunk sat in the hall, its brass worn at the edges. Dot caught her winter petticoat on it as she scuttled by.

The governess was in the parlour, sipping cold tea. Mistress Mary, her employer called her; it was to be understood that the Irish preferred this traditional form of address, and besides, it avoided the outlandish surname. Her Ladyship showed no interest in wages, nor in the little school Mistress Mary used to run in London, nor in her recent treatise on female education. Her Ladyship's questions sounded like statements. She outlined the children's day, hour by hour. They had been let run wild too long, and now it was a race to make the eldest presentable for Dublin Castle in a bare two years. The girl was somewhat perverse, her Ladyship mentioned over the silver teapot, and seemed to be growing larger by the day.

Mistress Mary watched a minute grain of powder from her Ladyship's widow's peak drift down and alight on the surface of the tea. She had been here one hour and felt light with fatigue already. The three children were the kind of hoydens she liked least, the fourteen-year-old Margaret in particular having an unrestrained guffaw certain to set on edge the nerves of any potential suitors. The governess asked herself again why she had exiled herself among the wild Irish rather than scour pots for a living.

'But your mother was a native of this country, was she not, Mistress Mary? You are half one of us, then.'

'Oh, your Ladyship, I would not presume.'

But that bony voice did remind the governess of her mother's limper tones. Bending her head over the tea, Mistress Mary heard in her gut the usual battle between gall and compassion.

Behind an oak, Margaret was shivering as she nipped her muslin skirts between her knees. If she stood narrow as a sapling she would not be seen. The outraged words of two languages carried across the field, equally indistinguishable. Dot would carry the news later: who said what, which of the usual threats and three-generation curses were made, which fists shaken in which faces. It had to be time for dinner, Margaret thought. She would go when the smoke rose white as feathers from the second thatch.

'Stand up straight,' her mother told her. 'You have been telling your sisters wicked make-believe once more. How can I persuade you of the difference between what is real and what is not?'

'I do not know madam.'

'You will run mad before the age of sixteen and then I will be spared the trouble of finding a husband for you.'

'Yes madam.'

'Have you forgotten who you are, girl?'

'Margaret King of the family of Lord and Lady Kingsborough of Kingsborough Estate.'

'Of which county?'

'Of the county of Cork in the kingdom of Ireland in the year of our Lord one thousand seven hundred and eighty six.'

'Now go and wash your face so your new governess will not think you a peasant.'

In November the evictions were more plentiful, and Margaret wearied of them. The apple trees stooped under their cloaks of rain. Mistress Mary had been here three weeks. She and the girls were kept busy all day from half past six to half past five with a list of nonsensical duties. So-called accomplishments being in her view those things which were never fully accomplished. Mistress Mary kept biting her soft lips and thinking of Lisbon. Between them the children churned out acres of lace, lists of the tributaries of the Nile, piles of netted purses, and an assortment of complaints from violin, flute, and harpsichord. The two small girls could sing five songs in French without understanding any of the words, and frequently did. The harpsichord was often silent, on days when Margaret, blank-faced and docile, slipped away with a message for the cook and was not seen again.

Sometimes, losing herself along windy corridors, her air of calm efficiency beginning to slip, Mistress Mary caught sight of a long booted ankle disappearing round a corner. On the first occasion, the matter was mentioned to her Ladyship. Bruises slowed Margaret's walk for a week, though no one referred to them. After that, Mistress Mary kept silent about her pupil's comings and goings. She would conquer the girl with kindness, she promised herself. Tenderness would lead where birch could not drive.

'Need the girl sleep in her stays, your Ladyship? She heaves so alarmingly at night when I look in on her . . . As your Ladyship wishes.'

Considering her governess's animated face bent over a letter, Margaret decided that here was one doll worth playing with. She knew how to do it. They always began stiff and proper but soon they went soft over you, and then every smile pulled their strings. Mostly they were lonely, and despised themselves for not being mothers. The Mademoiselle in her last boarding school was the easiest. Watch for the first signs – vague laughter, fingers against your cheek, a fuzziness about the hairline – and seize on her weakness. Ask her to help you tie the last bow of ribbon on your stomacher. Take her arm in yours while walking, beg to sit next

135

to her at supper, even bring her apples if the case requires it. Mademoiselle, the poor toad, had reached the stage of hiding pears in Margaret's desk.

By December, Mistress Mary was astonished at her power over this sweet little girl. The dreadful laugh had muted to a wheeze of merriment between wide lips. Margaret sat on a footstool below her governess's needle, and chanted French songs of which she understood half the words. At night, she had taken to pleading for Mistress Mary to come into her bedchamber; not Dot, nor any of the serving-maids, nor either of her sisters, only Mistress Mary might lift off the muslin cap and brush Margaret's long coarse hair. 'My little friend,' the woman called her, as a final favour, though when Margaret stood up she had a good inch over her governess. They shared a smile, then. Mistress Mary would have liked to be sure that they were smiling at the same thing.

Another thing the governess could not understand was why Margaret loved to read and hated to write.

Words were a treasure to be hoarded and never shared.

On Margaret's twelfth birthday two years before, an event marked only by one of her Ladyship's sudden visits to the schoolroom, she had been discovered sitting under a desk with a very blunt quill, writing 'The History of the Quintumbly Family, The Third Chapter'. Under interrogation in the parlour, Margaret could offer no reason for such an outlay of precious time. She licked the corner of her lips. Nor could she explain her knowledge of such an unsuitable family, who, it seemed, kept tame weasels and sailed down the Nile. Her Ladyship was disgusted at last to find that the Quintumblys were merely fanciful, a pretend family. The rest of the journal pleased her even less, being a daily account of Margaret's less filial thoughts and sentiments. Having read a sample of them aloud in a tone of wonder, her Ladyship picked

136

the limp book up by one corner and held it out to her daughter. Margaret was halfway to the parlour fire before her mother's voice tightened around her: did she mean to smoke them out entirely? Dot was called for to carry the manuscript to the gardener's bonfire, where it would do no harm.

From that day on the girl would write no words of her own, only lists of French verbs and English wars. In the strongbox behind her eyes, she stacked volumes of stories about her pretend families. She sealed her lashes and reread the adventures only in bed before it was light, in case anyone might catch her lips moving. By day she stole other people's words: romances, newspapers, treatises, anything left beside an armchair or in an unlocked cabinet in the library. Margaret swallowed up the words and would give none back.

Laid low by one of her periodic fevers in January, the girl was starving for a story but could not concentrate enough to form the letters. What she did remember to do was to clamour for Mistress Mary to hold her hand. The governess flushed, and consented, after a little show of reluctance. Humouring the patient, she agreed to petty things, like brushing her own dark hair with Margaret's ivory brush. By suppertime, the girl was too worn out to think of anything endearing to say, but Mistress Mary leaned over and hushed her most tenderly.

In her sleep, the girl made hoarse cries, and threw the gentlest hand off her forehead. 'There was a girl in Dublin used to sleep in her stays,' Dot remarked, 'that died from compunction of the organs.' The governess heaved a breath and knocked on the parlour door. 'Most dangerous in her state of health, your Ladyship . . . eminent medical gentlemen agree . . .' The stays came off. Margaret tossed still, picking at invisible ribbons across her chest.

The girl woke one February twilight to find that her lie had come true. She could not bear to let the governess out of her sight. Her puzzled eyes followed every movement, and her voice was cracked and fractious. She insisted that she could not remember how to sew. There was nothing comfortable about this love.

Scrawny children plucked at Margaret's skirts as she walked between the burnt cottages, wheezing. She shared her pocketful of French grapes among them. Their ginger freckles stood out bold on transparent skin.

Hungry for the familiarity of words, the girl stole into the library. She knelt on the moving steps and pressed her face against the glass cases, following their bevelled edges with her lips. One of the cases would be left unlocked, if she had prayed hard enough the night before. Titles in winking gold leaf reached for her fingers. At first she looked for storybooks and engravings, but by March she had got a taste for books of words about words: dictionaries and lexicons and medical encyclopedias. One strange fish of a word leapt into the mouth of another and that one into another, meanings hooked on each other, confusing and enticing her, until, after the hour or so she could steal from each day, Margaret was netted round with secret knowledge.

'There was a farmer went for the bailiff with a pitchfork last month,' Dot said. 'When they hanged him in Cork town his bit stuck up.' Margaret knew about bits and the getting of babies and the nine months; Mistress Mary, flushing slightly, said that every girl should know the words for things.

'Why was I not born a boy,' Margaret asked her governess while walking in the orchard, 'or why was I born at all?' Mistress Mary was bewildered by the question. Margaret explained: 'Girls are good for nothing in particular. In all the stories, boys can run and leap and save wounded animals. My mother says I am a mannish little trull. Already I am taller than ladies like you. So why may I not be a boy?'

'There is nothing wrong,' began Mistress Mary cautiously, 'with being manly, in the best sense. Manly virtues, you know, and masculine fortitude. You must not be afraid. No matter what anyone says. Even if they say things which, no doubt unintentionally, may seem unkind.'

Margaret kicked at a rotten apple.

'You must stand tall, like a tree,' explained the governess, gathering confidence. 'No matter how tall you grow you will be my little girl, and your head will always fit on my shoulder. Tall as a young tree,' she went on hurriedly, 'and you should move like one too. Why do you not romp and bound when I say you may; why do you cling to my side like a little doll?'

'My mother forbids it.'

'She cannot see through the garden wall. I give you permission.'

'She may ask why we spend so long in the orchard.'

'We are studying the names of the insects.'

And the governess tagged her on the shoulder and, picking up her skirts, hared off down a damp grassy path. Margaret was still considering the matter when she found her legs leaping away with her.

In the April evenings, Mistress Mary entertained the household with recitations and English country dances. Her Ladyship looked on, her hair whiter by the day. They argued over the number of buttons on the girls' boots.

When she grew up, Margaret had decided, she would make the bailiffs give all the rent back. The redheaded children would grow fat, and clap their hands when they saw her coming.

By May the air was white with blossom. Margaret could not swallow when she looked at her governess. Their hairs were

139

mingled on the brush; Margaret teased them with her cold fingers. She could not seem to learn the rules of bodies. What Mistress Mary called innocent caresses were allowable, and these were: cheeks and foreheads, lips on the backs of hands, arms entwined in the orchard, heads briefly nested in grey satin skirts. But when Margaret slipped into the governess's chamber one morning and found her in shift and stockings, she earned a scathing glance. Gross familiarity, Mistress Mary called it, and immodest forwardness. When she had fastened her last button and called the girl back into the room, she explained more calmly that one must never forget the respect which one human creature owed another. Margaret could not see what respect had to do with dressing in separate rooms. She hung her head and thought of breakfast.

'Has any of the servants ever tried to teach you dirty indecent tricks?'

'No, Mistress Mary. Dot is always busy, and besides, she knows no tricks.'

It was June by the time she found that there were words for girls like her. Words tucked away in the library, locked only until you looked for them. *Romp* and *hoyden* she knew already. *Tomboy* was when she ran down the front staircase with her bootlaces undone. But there were sharper words as well, words that cut when she lifted them into her mouth to taste and whisper them. *Tommie* was when women kissed and pressed each other to their hearts, it said so in a dirty poem on the top shelf of the cabinet. *Tribad* was the same only worse. The word had to mean, she reasoned, along the lines of *triangle* and *trimester*, that she was three times as bad as other girls.

Margaret knelt up on the moving steps as the page fell open to that word again; her legs shook and her belly-rumbles echoed under the whalebone. *Tribad* meant if she let the badness take her, she would grow and grow. Already she was taller than anyone in the house except her mother. The book said she would grow down there until she became a hermaphrodite shown for pennies at the fair, or ran away in her brother's breeches (but she had no brother) and married a Dutch widow. The change was coming already. When the girl lay in bed on hot mornings the bit between her legs stirred and leapt like a minnow.

One noon she limped into the bedchamber, phantom blows from her mother's rod still landing on her calves. Dot was sweeping the cold floor, her broom trailing now as she gazed into the frontispiece of a book of travels.

'Give it,' said Margaret.

Dot regarded her, then stared at the book again, at its pages flattened by the grey morning light. She looked back at the girl as if trying to remember her name. Seizing the besom, Margaret threaded her fingers between the twigs, and set to bludgeoning the maid's thick body with the handle. The coarse petticoats dulled the impact; it sounded like a rug being beaten. She pursued Dot to the window with a constant hiss of phrases, from 'idle ignoramus' to 'tell my mother' to 'dirty goodfornothing inch of life'. Dot broke into a wail at last, expressive less of pain than of a willingness to get it over and done with. She stood in the corner, hunched over to protect her curves. Tears plummeted to the floorboards.

'Beg pardon,' Margaret instructed. Her ribs heaved and sank under the creaking corset.

'Beg pardon miss,' Dot repeated, her tone neutral.

The broom was lowered but the eyes held.

Margaret had made it to the door before, with a lurch, she found herself sorry. She turned to see Dot industriously brushing her tears into the floor. She was so sorry it swamped her, left her feeble. Was there any comfort to give? A lump in one of the unmade beds reminded her, and she scrabbled under the

141

coverlet. The doll she pulled out was missing one eye, but her pink damask slippers were good as new. The girl walked up behind Dot and tapped her on the shoulder with the doll's powdered head. 'Take her,' she said graciously, 'and leave off crying.'

Dot turned a face that was almost dry. 'What am I to do with that, miss?'

Margaret was disconcerted. Play with her, she could have said, but when? Dress her up, but in what? A shaky, benevolent smile. 'Perhaps you could beat her when you are angry.'

Weary, Dot considered the two faces. 'Get away out of that, miss,' she remarked at last, and walked from the room, trailing her broom behind her.

It was in the corner of the bedchamber that the governess found the girl a little later, her fingers dividing and dividing the doll's hair. She lifted Margaret's hands away gently. 'Girl, you harass my spirits. You are too old for your sisters' dolls, and what need has a healthy girl of wax toys when there is the wide world to play in?' If she noticed the stiffness in Margaret's legs, as they strolled in the orchard, she said nothing. They spoke of birds' nests, and poetry, and unrest among the French.

Mistress Mary had taken to writing a story in the bright July evenings. What was it about? 'Disappointment,' she murmured, and would tell no more. Feeling neglected, Margaret became clumsier, tripping over shoes and toppling an inkstand. The governess forgave her everything. One morning Margaret found a double cherry hung over the handle of her wardrobe. She knew she had the power now. It brought her no joy.

'I govern her completely,' Mistress Mary wrote to her sister. 'She is a fine girl, and it only takes a cherry to win a smile from her. Her violence of temper remains deplorable, but I myself never feel the effects of it. She is wax in my hands. The truth is,

142

this girl is the only consolation of my life in this backwater. How I look forward to my brief escape!'

Nobody remembered to tell the children that their governess was spending two days with acquaintances in Tralee. Distracted by the details of mailcoaches and hats, Mistress Mary was gone before breakfast. Dot, passing the girl on the back staircase, had only time to whisper that the governess was gone.

Margaret stood in the middle of the empty bedchamber. Sure enough, Mistress Mary's travelling cloak was missing for the first time since October. Margaret was oddly calm. Her mind was busy wondering what she had done wrong, what brief immodesty or careless phrase would make her governess punish her so, by leaving without a word. She noticed that the writing case had been left behind. No reason not to, now: she wrenched it open and took a handful of pages. 'Pity is one of my prevailing passions', she read, and 'this world is a desert to me' at the top of another leaf. For a few moments the girl stood, savouring the grandeur of the phrases. But then they were dust in her mouth. All these words, and not an inch of warm skin left. As if Mistress Mary, who had never seemed too fond of having a body, had escaped in the form of a bird or a cloud.

The words were building up behind her tongue, making her gag. Nine months she has been living behind my hair, thought Margaret; that is as long as a baby. She parted her lips to breathe and a howl split her open.

After that she remembered nothing until her mother was standing over her.

'Stop this fuss,' her Ladyship advised. 'You are making a grand calamity out of nothing at all. Recollect yourself. Who are you?'

'I don't know.'

'You are Margaret King, of . . . ?'

'I don't remember.'

The girl stood, at the rod's pleasure. It beat and beat and could not touch her.

Due to the excessive regret the girl had shown at the briefest of partings with her governess, her Ladyship explained to the household, she had decided that Mistress Mary would not be coming back. The black trunk was sent off before breakfast.

By August, Margaret was bleeding inside. Feeling herself seep away, she was not surprised. But Dot saw the red path down the girl's stocking; she took her into a closet and explained the business of the rags. Margaret nodded but did not believe her. She knew it was the first sign of the change. Blood had to trickle as the growth sped and the new freakish flesh pushed through. When she was three inches long, she would run away to Galway fair and show herself for sixpences. The pretend families would come with her, riding in the ropes of her hair.

A Republican in 1798, Margaret would spit at bailiffs. Later, an adulteress in Italy, she would meet her governess's daughter, who never knew her mother, and would tell her, 'I knew your mother.'

Note

One of the puzzles of Mary Wollstonecraft's early career is her losing her job as governess with the Kingsborough family in Cork. For 'Words for Things', I have drawn on her *Collected Letters* (1979), but also her *Thoughts on the Education of Daughters* (1787), *Mary, A Fiction* (1788), and *A Vindication of the Rights of Woman* (1792). The character of 'Mademoiselle' was inspired by Mary Russell Mitford's 'Early Recollections: The French Teacher' in *Our Village* (1826).

Wollstonecraft's pupil became Margaret King Moore on her marriage to the second Earl of Mount Cashell, to whom she bore eight children. The British Library has a letter from Bishop Percy to his wife in 1798 which mentions Margaret's vigorous defence of her former governess when Wollstonecraft was accused of being a bad influence on her charges. In 1805, Margaret eloped from her husband and children with George William Tighe; in Italy, they became friends with the daughter Wollstonecraft died giving birth to, Mary Shelley.

How a Lady Dies

Breathing hardly seems worth the trouble today. Elizabeth lets out her shallow mouthful of air. Her shoulders subside; her head sinks back against the obelisk. She stares up at the tapering stone, but the sight dizzies her. Her eyelids fall. Fur is soft against her cheekbones.

There, between the breaths, is peace. A little more air seeps away between her withered lips. The forest inside her ribs is emptying. No sound, nothing stirring, no fear, nor inclination. How the end will come. This winter, surely. Perhaps this very month. Could it be today?

This is all she has to do, thinks Elizabeth with a sudden inspiration. No vulgar act of self-destruction is called for; nothing to trouble her conscience or her taste. It is necessary only to relinquish: the daily effort, the stale cold air.

Her whole self hisses away through the crack of her mouth. Her stomach gives a startling rumble. She feels it fold in on itself. Soon she will be quite hollowed out. The weight on her chest grows, but she tells herself not to tremble, not to resist, not to bother with another breath.

'Elizabeth?'

The voice of love is a noose. It keeps you dangling between two worlds.

Her lungs suck in a huge mouthful of air. Her stays crack mightily, like a ship turning into the wind. How this worthless body fights for life. She turns to see her friend's anxious face, cooped up in a silk bonnet. Dark eyes, a high forehead traced like paper. By the world's standards, a plain woman, twenty years past her best. 'I am only resting, my dear,' Elizabeth murmurs.

'Do you feel a little better in yourself today?' suggests Frances. 'Indeed,' faintly.

The only thing one can do in Bath that one did not do the day before is die. This is the undisputed bon mot of the season of 1759. Mrs Montagu's words will be misquoted long after these swarms of visitors have dispersed to their respective altars and graves.

Every year more yellowstone houses seize their share of tawny light. Every day more carriages scurry across the valley. Each duke married off is replaced by another five; every beggar arrested leaves room for fifty more. What was once a gracious maiden of a town has become a bloated dowager.

Bath is known for social rules and hard drinking, exquisite refinement and filthy jokes. Money is the air it breathes. Half a guinea to the Bellringers to herald your arrival, another to the City Waits for the obligatory serenade, then two guineas' subscription to Harrison's Rooms, where the tea is only ever lukewarm. People come to Bath to take the waters, but also to take the air in the Orange Grove, to take heart at the sight of a handsome face. They take their turns at scandal and glory, pleasure and spleen; they take their time about living and dying. The town is full of sound lungs proclaiming their sickness, old men insisting on their youth, married women whispering their unhappiness.

'That's Miss Pennington,' the gossips say; 'she does not dance.' Which, in Bath code, means: spare your breath. Her partner is bony and invisible. The lady's not for marrying.

Miss Elizabeth Pennington is a fortune, past twenty-five and still a spinster. Friends blame her health. Enemies blame her finickiness. She has come to Bath in the care of a humble companion, Mrs Sheridan. ('Wife to the theatre man, don't you know, with a houseful of children left at home.') Both ladies are vicar's daughters, but there the resemblance ends. The younger has all the money, it is said, and the elder all the wit.

What the gossips don't know is that a year ago, Elizabeth turned up on her friend's doorstep in Covent Garden without a word of warning. 'I am come to take up my abode with you,' she stuttered, absurdly Biblical. Words memorised in the hired carriage, sentences stiff with anticipated disappointment.

'I find it impossible to live without you.'

She strained for a breath.

'You may shut your doors against me—'

The doors swung open.

She lived all that year with Frances and her Mr Sherry and her children. Elizabeth taught the smaller ones Aesop's fables, poured tea for Sherry's visitors, and could always be relied upon to have read their latest works. When the new baby came, the Sheridans named her Betsy, in Elizabeth's honour.

She made sure to make herself indispensable. Sherry joked that his wife had no need of his company any more; he stayed out late with poets and ballet-masters. In letters from home, the Reverend Pennington asked his daughter with increasing querulousness how long her friend would require her. Elizabeth answered only with remarks on the weather.

She picked at her food, and fed the best bits to the baby. Whenever she was taken by a coughing fit, that long winter, she covered her mouth with one of her two dozen handkerchiefs, each of them trimmed with the best Bruges lace.

Frances refused to be alarmed by her friend's husky voice, the violet tinge about her eyes. All her darling Elizabeth needed was a trip to Bath: taking the waters and seeing the sights would restore anyone to perfect health. Especially one so young. Especially one so worthy of all life held in store.

And what could Sherry do but agree? What husband could object, except a brute? What could any man say, who had the slightest sense of the exquisite force of female friendship?

They promised to write to him weekly. They left the baby with a good clean nurse.

Before dawn Elizabeth is shaken awake by the rattle of carts, the bawling of muffin-men.

'I declare,' yawns Frances beside her in a perfect imitation of Lady Danebury, 'this is such a *fatigating* life, I scarce have strength to rise!'

This town was designed by the sick; every hour a different amusement keeps death at bay. At sunrise they go to the Bath in sedan chairs; the chairmen's puffing breaths leave white trails on the air. The first time Elizabeth saw a bathing costume, she was so appalled she laughed out loud, but now she pulls on the yellow canvas jacket and petticoat and thinks nothing of it. What she shrinks from is the moment of ducking under the arch and wading out into the basin, under the grey sky. The water scalds, even on the coldest mornings. Elizabeth cannot help imagining that she is being boiled down to the bone, rendered into soup.

Oblivious to the heat that flushes their cheeks, ladies stand and gossip with their necessaries laid out on little floating trays: snuffboxes, pomanders, nosegays wilting fast. Clouds of yellow steam fill the air. In a far corner, Frances has her bad leg pumped on. She chats with the pump-man as if he were family; she lacks any sense of the gulf between herself and the lower orders. Elizabeth can always make out her friend's voice in a crowd; still full of Dublin, after all these years.

Two boys dive in, raising wings of water. Elizabeth holds down her stiff skirts so no one can snatch at them. She tells herself that no one is looking at her, but lodgings crowd around the Bath, and footmen and beggars ring the walls, pointing out the fairest faces, the greatest dowries. One day someone threw a cat in, and there was a wonder: it could swim.

Elizabeth backs against a pillar, light-headed. She pulls her handkerchief from her straw hat to wipe her cheeks. She sinks deeper into the water, and fiery fingers lay hold of her stiff shoulders; for a moment she is relieved to the point of tears. She shuts her eyes and tells herself to trust in the waters. So many, of all ranks of life, have been cured, even some three times her age; there is a marble cross in the corner, hung with discarded crutches. Why can she not believe?

It seems to her now that these are the waters of death in which disease leaks from one frail body to another. The ghostly smell of bad eggs fills up her nostrils, and a stained plaster floats by. Flakes of snow drift down from the sky, then turn to rain; the whole world is made of vapour.

'My dearest?'

That smile that sustains her, like daily bread.

When Elizabeth climbs up the steps to join Frances, her costume weighs on her so she cannot breathe. But then again, she cannot remember when she last drew breath without a struggle. When she was a girl? A child? At home, there was an oak tree; surely she climbed it?

The Guides are stained brown from the waters. They tell her how well she looks today. Such a lie is worth half a crown each.

The leather of the sedan chair is still wet from the last customer. 'Home now, and quick about it, before Miss Pennington takes cold!' orders Mrs Sheridan. Her voice is sharp with borrowed authority. But she has omitted to tip the chair-man in advance; she finds it hard to persuade herself to make free with her young friend's fortune. Out of spite the man leaves the curtains open, so the rain drifts in on Elizabeth's eyelids. The streets are clogged with barrows.

Back in bed, the ladies keep the blankets over their heads to make themselves sweat out the poisons. Outside the muddy window, the pattens strapped to strangers' feet clink like blackbirds. To distract her friend from the cough that doubles her up, Frances recites some new phrases she overheard in the Bath. 'My dear girl is *vastly* embellished, she is a perfect *progeny* of learning,' she squeaks. 'La, my dear, you put me in a terrible *agility*!'

Lying there, chuckling and wheezing, Elizabeth should be perfectly happy. She is happier, at least, than she has ever been in her short and narrow life. Is she not here, in Bath, with Frances, the two of them curtained in their bed, forgetting fathers and husbands and children and all, shedding the ordinary world?

By eight in the morning the ladies are at the Pump Room, listening to the violins and forcing down the water.

Words fill the air around them like feathers, moving too fast to catch. 'Your lordship's immensely good.' 'I'm laced so tight my stomach's sore.' 'Nay, I grant you, the fellow dresses prodigiously.' 'Oh, lud!' 'Oh, monstrous!' 'Miss Pennington? La, she'll not last till Easter.'

Elizabeth lowers her eyes and sips her glass of warm metallic water. For a moment she has the impression she is drinking blood. Frances must have overheard that remark too; she gets two red spots high on her cheeks, and tells her young friend how

151

becoming her lavender pelisse is, and her little muff of rabbit-skin.

Elizabeth knows better, knows what Frances cannot know, must never find out. She knows she wants to die.

The doctors think a young lady of fortune must have everything to live for. Each doctor who visits assures her that he knows where to fix the blame: frailty in the family, damp in the bones, tight-lacing and spiced food, an excess of exercise or education, too many baths. One recommends enemas; another, marriage. Miss Pennington thanks them all and pays their fees without a murmur. She is coming to realise how very rich she is. If she was only a pauper, this dying would be over with long ago.

At Mr Leake's booksellers Elizabeth and Frances browse through the latest poems about the antiquities of Bath and the pleasures of melancholy. But they like the old books best. Sometimes they spend the morning on a sofa, reading aloud their favourite letters from their dear Mr Richardson's *Clarissa*. Elizabeth often asks Frances for the scene in which Anna comes to see her dead Clary's body. 'My sweet clay-cold friend,' Anna cries, trying to kiss some heat back into the corpse; 'my sweet clay-cold friend, awake.'

Halfway through that letter, Frances glances up from the page to rest her ageing eyes, and for a moment her gaze admits it. Acknowledges that Elizabeth is not simply ailing, not simply weak in her spirits. Truth flickers in the air between the two of them. And then Frances snaps the book shut and remarks, 'How well that yellow lace becomes you!'

Elizabeth loves her most for the lies.

Frances hopes one day to write a novel. The heroine will meet unhappiness on every page, but she will never stop being good. She has never mentioned it to Sherry; she would prefer to surprise him. Elizabeth is the only one to know of her plan.

It occurs to Elizabeth that her friend is misled by the younger woman's pale, slim face, her gentle expression, her occasional verses. An unmarried, invalid lady is too easily assumed to be all soul, all sweetness. Frances seems to think that because the good suffer in this imperfect world, those who suffer must be good. Has she never peered into the back of Elizabeth's eyes and seen the greed, the rage, the morbid longings? How well does she know her friend, for all her devotion?

Elizabeth cannot face the public breakfast, held every morning at eleven. On good days, Frances may prevail upon her to visit a pastry-cook's for a jelly or a tart. Elizabeth always tries a bite or two, then lays her spoon down unobtrusively and pushes the plate towards her friend, an inch at a time. Frances takes mouthfuls between her eager sentences.

They might try on hats at a milliner's, or visit the ladies' coffee house, where Elizabeth sips the sweet black brew till the dizziness retreats to a distance. If the day is mild and the gutters stink, they buy violets to hold to their noses. They cross the path of the same people five times a day, with a curtsey for each, like nodding marionettes. There's Mr Allen, noted for benevolence; Mr Quin, once the king of the stage; Mr Gainsborough, whose rooms are stuffed with handsome ladies and their handsomer portraits.

Red-faced servants trundle wheelchairs up and down the streets. Elizabeth avoids the eyes of the desiccated women who let themselves be rolled along. But then she makes herself give one of them a civil nod. She need not stiffen at the creak of a wheelchair; she need have no fear, for herself, of such a drawn-out old age.

Down by the river, the ladies stand and look across at the sweet wooded curves in the distance. 'Someday we'll drive to the hills,'

153

says Frances. 'When you are feeling more like yourself.'

If Elizabeth can catch a breath today, she and Frances will walk up to see the Circus. Mr Wood is always there, overseeing the buildings his father dreamed of; this will be the first street in the world to form a perfect circle. He points out where the tiers of Doric columns will rise, where the Ionic, where the Corinthian. The ladies smile with their mouths shut, so as not to yawn. Elizabeth tries to imagine being needed by the world, having such projects, reasons to stay alive.

The wind pours down North Parade and soaks right through her. The air moves past her mouth too fast for her lips to catch. She stands still, waiting for a breath to come her way, utterly insubstantial. It occurs to her that she died some weeks ago and never noticed. Perhaps she is not the only one. Perhaps the whole city is populated with ghosts, and their faces are made of powder, and their hooped skirts are empty as bells.

'Race you to the bottom of the hill,' says Frances with light irony. Elizabeth starts to laugh, soundlessly. She slides her arm into the elder's and offers her whole weight. Interlocked, they set off on the infinitely slow walk down.

Everyone goes to the Abbey at noon. Above the great door, stone angels on ladders climb to heaven and let themselves down to earth. Joyous and polite, they wait their turn, even the ones whose heads have been worn away by centuries of rain.

Elizabeth and Frances like to sit at the back. Bright coloured light drips through the windows. Today the sermon is on Gethsemane. *Then saith he unto them, My soul is exceeding sorrowful, even unto death; tarry ye here, and watch with me.*

Her pale hand and her friend's brown-spotted one lie together on the pew. *What, could ye not watch with me one hour?* She steals a look at Frances, her serious profile, the drag of the skin

154

around her eyes. The church is full of people, but for Elizabeth the world has narrowed to one face.

Watch and pray, that ye enter not into temptation: the spirit indeed is willing, but the flesh is weak.

If Elizabeth feels up to it, she argues with her Creator. Her illness, she tells Him, is none of her making. But this is only partly true, and she knows it. True, in Elizabeth's lungs, there is a sickness like a dreadful guest who sits and sits and will not leave. But in her heart squats the sickness that will not let her eat, will not let her live. Not long, at any rate. No longer than this companionship will be permitted to last; no longer than she may wake every morning to the soft nape of Frances's neck.

Her favourite part of the day is when they linger after the service and read the memorial tablets.

> *Thro' painful suff'rings, tranquil to the last,*
> *Thy lips no murmurs, no repinings passed . . .*

Some are in the shape of urns, bulging like stomachs from the wall; others are fallen columns.

> *In testimony of regard to the memory*
> *of a pearl beyond price,*
> *this monument is erected*
> *by her much afflicted husband.*

One tablet is meant to be a curtain; the marble ripples beneath the letters.

> *A woman truly amiable . . .*
> *translated into another world . . .*

155

'This one lived to the age of ninety-two,' marvels Frances.

Elizabeth leans over her friend's shoulder. Their cheeks are not an inch apart. What she has never explained to Frances is that she is choosing phrases for her own inscription.

> *. . . though sudden to her friends yet not to her,*
> *as appears by these verses*
> *found in her closet after her decease . . .*

No, Elizabeth has written nothing worth marble. Her verses are thin leaden things. Nothing to leave behind her, then. Only a share in a much-divided heart.

> *. . . but to none could her merits be so well known*
> *as to her affectionate friend,*
> *who considered her as her support,*
> *her comfort and advisor . . .*

'Here comes Mr Lampton,' hisses Frances in her ear, 'and we've still not called on his mother.'

> *. . . whose grief must be as lasting as breath . . .*

But how lasting is that? Elizabeth leans on a pew, wheezing. Darkness comes and goes about her eyes.

'My dear? Are you ill?' asks Frances.

> *. . . who henceforth can look to no happiness*
> *but in the hope of reunion*
> *with the dear departed in a happier world.*

156

That is the thought Elizabeth clings to. The other world, the only real world, when she and Frances will have outrun time. When need and guilt and incomprehension will have fallen away like hairs from a brush. Where the two friends may stroll for ever between soft green trees.

They dine at three. How sweet, the press of a worried hand on one's wrist. But eating seems inconceivable. Elizabeth's mouth will only open the width of a finger, and the beef smells of blood. She has the impression that wine drains through her as the rain through peat; that food is too slippery to glue itself to her bones. If her friend bullies her to eat, tears begin to collect in her plate.

'Oh my dear, my dear!'

The ladies sip port to celebrate the anniversary of their meeting. They forget to write to Sherry and the children. Elizabeth feels a terrible delight.

At five they go to the Theatre, or to Harrison's Rooms. Lady Cholmondley complains about the servants. 'The very teeth in one's head aren't safe, if one sleeps with one's mouth open!' Every table has a literary lady or two. There sits Mrs Scott, a little pockmarked authoress who lives at Batheaston with a female friend. It is said her husband tried to poison her before she ran away from him. 'She is much to be *compassionated*, poor soul . . .'

For a moment, sipping her thin tea, Elizabeth lets herself imagine Sherry as a murderer. As a man who deserves to have his wife stolen away from him, before he wears her out with bearing a dozen children. But having lived in his house all year, observed his kindness and his chatter, Elizabeth knows the worst that can be said is that he is a bit of a bore. He has never seen his wife for the wonder she is; he has no idea of his luck.

Every other lady's friend is content with her share, she reminds

157

herself, biting down on the frail edge of her cup. What would the world come to if they asked for more?

There is a Dress Ball each evening at six. Elizabeth refuses every gentleman who asks her: 'I regret my health does not permit . . .' Two hours of minuets, then an hour of old-style country dances; the young ladies go off to remove their hoops so as not to bruise themselves. Frances taps her foot and says it is not proper for a married lady to dance. Elizabeth always overcomes her friend's objections by the end of the evening. She smiles as she watches the older woman whirl across the floor with one widower after another.

But every night feels like the last night. Elizabeth sucks the marrow of pleasure out of each hour like a starving dog. This cannot go on.

'Quadrille!' cries Lord Humphry.

'Ombre,' contradicts his sister.

Now the ladies look on, and fan themselves; the rooms are airless. Elizabeth watches Frances out of the corner of her eye. She knows there are limits to what a friend may ask, even the dearest of friends. She knows their stay was never meant to last so long. Any day now, Elizabeth must let Frances go home to her family, to the baby she will barely recognise. This is where the story ends.

When the gaming is over, there is an auction at which an Ethiopian girl sells for five guineas. 'Vastly amusing,' shrieks her new owner. Elizabeth meets the small milky eyes of the child and feels all at once that she may faint. Blackness covers her like a cloth thrown over a birdcage.

Frances rushes her home at once, with a link-boy stumbling ahead with his torch. They pass two women in bleached aprons. 'Harlots,' whispers Frances in her friend's ear. Elizabeth clings to her arm. Her breath echoes in the narrow street.

*   *   *

158

In, out, so regular, so unstoppable. Elizabeth tries to match her own breathing to her friend's. She turns painfully on her side and watches Frances's face in the moonlight that leaks through the window, across the pillow. Soft lines score the lofty forehead: a face worn out with feeling. Who does Frances love? Her spendthrift Sherry, her big Tom, her Charlie-boy, her Dick the Dunce, her pretty Lissy, her baby Betsy . . . How can she have any love left? Yet it seems to come as easy as sweat. She even manages to love Elizabeth, this dry husk of womanhood lying beside her, bitter, unsleeping. *Sister of my heart*, she calls her, sometimes.

But the latest letter from Sherry is under the pillow. Elizabeth read it by candlelight while Frances was downstairs shouting at the chambermaid to fetch a compress for Miss Pennington's chest. Her hand shook as she opened the letter; she almost set the edge on fire. One word told her all she needed: 'Dublin'.

The friends have had their season.

I find it impossible to live without you. If Frances were to wake now, this minute, and ask her, look her in the eye and ask, 'What is the matter with you?' – that is all Elizabeth could say, like a child repeating her one lesson.

I find it impossible to live.

She cannot remember how she got through the days before Bath, before London, how she bore the weight of her short life without Frances to share it. And still less can she conceive of how she is to live, in a week or a month or two at most, when Frances and her family will go back to Dublin.

Impossible.

A rough sea, a universe away.

She coughs, stifling it in the pillow. Then she lets herself cough louder. If she sounds bad enough, the older woman will wake from her shallow sleep and tend to her. She will stroke her friend's forehead, cluck over her tenderly. If Elizabeth coughs hard enough to wet the pillow, Frances will surely kiss her face. If she stays awake all night, she will look even paler in the morning, and Frances will scold her and coddle her and bring her hot wine. If she cannot breathe, in the bad time before dawn, Frances will lift her in her own arms and count her breaths for her.

As long as she keeps getting worse, Frances will stay.

Such thoughts, such weakness. Is it her body that's diseased or her mind? In the dark, Elizabeth cannot remember how to be good. How do they endure, those heroines of novels? A tear burns its way through her lashes.

Today she is weaker than yesterday, when she was weaker than the day before. She's eaten nothing to speak of for a fortnight. Sitting in the Abbey at noon, Elizabeth's eyes drift up the walls, across the floor. Every inch is inscribed; the place is crowded with names, packed tight like a gala ball for the dead.

She glides out of her stiff body, slips through the stained glass windows, soars up into the aromatic streets. She hovers round the Abbey, grips with one white smoky hand the stone ladder that the blunt-toed angels are climbing. She watches, she waits. How will it be?

She sees Frances roaming the streets, the ribbons of her bonnet hanging loose. Forgetful of her family, red-eyed for a year, heart-sore for the rest of her life. Frances, transformed into a greedy girl on the doorstep of Heaven, knocking furiously, ready to make her demands.

Even within the dream, Elizabeth feels the implausibility of this. Suddenly she can see another Frances, a grey-haired Frances, revisiting Bath, only a little melancholy when she glances down South Parade to the stone bench where she used to sit with 'poor Miss Pennington'. And all around the visitor, the barrows and stalls and colliding sedan chairs, the nittigritties of Bath life going on just as ever, oblivious to the words etched on marble in the Abbey.

Elizabeth comes back to the present, to a warm hand wrapping itself around hers. This is what it comes down to: a firm grip that banishes past and future.

Feeling a tickle in her lungs she withdraws her fingers apologetically, searching for her handkerchief. No one turns a head; racking coughs are no novelty in Bath. But Elizabeth stares into her snowy handkerchief at the bold red flag death has planted there.

She folds it over and over till only white shows.

Not yet. Please. I did not mean, I did not know, I thought— Impossible.

Down the aisle, her heels resounding. Scandalised whispers on every side. 'What ill-breeding, to run off from church!'

I am only twenty-five.

She bursts through the great double doors of the Abbey as if they were veils. Out in the watery sunshine, she takes a great breath. And another.

Frances is at her elbow.

Elizabeth presses her fingers against her friend's hot mouth before she can say a word. 'We have so little time,' she whispers.

Tonight, Miss Pennington will dance.

Note

'How a Lady Dies' is about Elizabeth Pennington, born in 1732 or 1734, a wealthy vicar's daughter who wrote poetry, most of which has been lost. Her closest friend was the writer Frances Sheridan (1724–66). Sometime in the 1750s Elizabeth turned up on Frances's doorstep to say she could not live without her, as recorded in Alice Lefanu, *Memoirs of the Life and Writings of Mrs Frances Sheridan* (1824). I have drawn on a letter by Frances in John Watkins's *Memoirs of the Public and Private Life of the Right Honourable Richard Brinsley Sheridan* (1817), as well as her comedy *A Journey to Bath* (written in 1764).

On their return from Bath to London, Elizabeth died in Frances's arms.

A Short Story

Formed in her mother's belly, dark filigree: the watermark of the bones.

The birth was easy. She glided out easy as a minnow into the slipstream of life. The midwife crossed herself. The mother wept with gratitude for this Thumbelina, this daughter of her mind's eye, embodied on the bloody sheet. The father wept with dread to see what he had spawned. Seven inches long, one pound in weight.

Hold it. Linger on the picture. Here, before poverty and ambition began to pose their questions, before strangers started knocking on the door, before the beginning of the uneasy vigil which would last four years. Here for one moment, silence in the small hot room in Cork: a private wonder.

Mr and Mrs Crackham named their daughter Kitty.

She could not be said to have had a childhood. Her whole life was lived in proportion to her body, that is, in miniature; infancy, youth and adulthood passed as rapidly as clouds across the sun. She was never exactly strong, in her body or her head; she was never exactly well. But Kitty Crackham did have pleasures to match her pains; she liked bright colours, and fine clothes, and if she heard music she would tap the floor with her infinitesimal foot.

At three years old she was one foot seven inches tall, and seemed to have given up growing. She never spoke, and the cough shook her like a dog. Doctor Gilligan assured the Crackhams that the air of England was much more healthful to children than that of Ireland, especially in tubercular cases such as little Kitty's. He offered to take her over the sea himself. He mentioned, only in passing, the possibility of introducing the child to certain men of science and ladies of quality. A select audience; the highest motives: to further the cause of physiological knowledge. It might help somewhat to defray the costs of her keep, he added.

Such kindness from a virtual stranger!

The Crackhams packed their daughter's tiny bag and sent her off with Doctor Gilligan, but not before he'd given them three months' rent.

Later they wished they'd said no. Later still, they wished they'd asked for twice as much. They had four other children, all full-size, all hungry.

The child was silent on the coach to Dublin, and on the ship too, even when the waves stood up like walls. The Doctor couldn't tell if she was weak-witted, or struck dumb by loss. Certainly, she was no ordinary girl. Their fellow-travellers gasped and pointed as the Doctor carried Kitty Crackham along the deck in the crook of his arm. He pulled up her hood; it irked him that all these gawkers were getting a good look for free.

After dinner, when he'd thrown up the last of his lamb chops, his mind cleared. It struck him that the girl's tininess would seem even more extraordinary if she were, say, nine years old instead of three. To explain her speechlessness, he could present her as an exotic foreigner. By the time they docked, he'd taught her to stagger towards him whenever he called *Caroline*.

* * *

164

It was Caroline Crachami, the Dwarf from Palermo, who landed at Liverpool in the year 1823: 'the smallest of all persons mentioned in the records of littleness', the Doctor's pamphlet boasted. In a fanciful touch he was rather proud of, the pamphlet suggested that her growth had been blighted in the womb by a monkey that had bitten Signora Crachami's finger.

The first exhibition, at Liverpool, drew barely a trickle of punters, but Doctor Gilligan forced himself to be patient. On to Birmingham, where the crowd began to swell, then Oxford. Town after town, room after room, month after month. Each of the child's days was crammed with strangers so big they could have crushed her with an accidental step. Such excitement in the eyes of these Brobdingnagians, now their Gulliver had come at last. Some called her *she*, others, *it*. Dr Gilligan took to wearing a Sicilian moustache; and calling her *my darling daughter*.

She made her audiences doubt their senses and cry out in delight. How strong she made them feel – but also, how clumsy. They could hardly bear to think of a child being so small and brittle, so they called her the Sicilian Fairy. As if a newborn baby had risen magically from her cradle and dressed herself to parade before them; as if her powers were in inverse proportion to her size, and she could fly out of any danger! She was the doll they had always wished would come to life.

In London Doctor Gilligan tested the weight of his moneybags and hired an exhibition room in Bond Street. He provided his *darling daughter* with a tiny ring, thimble-cup and bed. She sat on a tea-caddy that served her for a throne. He taught her to take a bit of biscuit from his hand, then rub her stomach and say 'Good, good.' He was delighted when after a week or two she began to talk a little more, as it increased the entertainment. 'Papa,' she called him, without much prompting. She had a faint high voice, not of this world, and visitors had to stoop to hear her; the Doctor repeated everything she said, adding a few touches of his own.

For a foreign child, people said, she was a quick learner of English. She put her hand over her mouth when she felt a cough coming, and she tottered across the deep carpets as if always about to drop. She was seen to express emotions of various kinds, such as gratitude, irritation, mirth, and panic.

The Doctor was less pleased when his measurements showed that she had grown a quarter of an inch.

Caroline Crachami was now one foot eight inches tall – still, by a good thirteen inches, the smallest female on record. The papers called her the Nation's Darling, the Wonder of Wonders. The King took her hand between his finger and thumb, and declared himself immensely pleased to make her acquaintance. He sat her on his footstool and had her thimble filled with a drop of his best port. She coughed and whooped and all the ladies laughed.

After that the crowds swelled and multiplied. Three hundred of the nobility visited her, three thousand of the quality, and as many of the lower sort as could beg, borrow or steal the price of admission. Gentlemen adored Miss Crachami. Ladies grew jealous, began to call her powdery and withered.

For an extra shilling Miss Crachami could be handled. When sceptical Grub Street men came in, Dr Gilligan invited them to handle her for free. One gentleman with a stubbled chin picked her up in one hand – she only weighed five pounds – and kissed her. She was seen to wriggle away and wipe her face. He got a highly amusing article out of the episode. Readers were assured that there was every probability of this Progeny of Nature living to an advanced age.

* * *

166

But nothing about Caroline Crachami took long, and her death was particularly quick. That Thursday in June she received more than two hundred visitors. A little languor was noted, and was only to be expected; a little rattle when she coughed. In the coach on the way back to their Duke Street lodgings, while Doctor Gilligan was looking out the window, she dropped soundlessly to the floor and died.

He assumed she was only in a faint. He couldn't believe it was all over.

Given the Doctor's commitment to the furthering of physiological knowledge, what came next was no surprise. He carried the body round to all the anatomists and finally sold it to the Royal College of Surgeons.

Doctor Clift was not the kind of doctor who offered cures. He was an articulator; a butcher in the service of science, or even art. His job was to draw grace and knowledge out of putridity. He needed a delicate touch in this case, as the carcass was so small.

First he cut it open, and learned what he could from the spotted lungs and shrunken organs. Then he chopped the body into convenient and logical sections, just like jointing a hen or a rabbit, and boiled it down. For several days he stirred this human soup and let it stew; finally he poured it away, leaving only the greasy bones. He'd got inured to the smell thirty years ago.

Odd, he thought, that the same people who would retch at the stench of such a soup would line up to drink in the sight of the same bones, once he had strung them together. Such was his artistry. It was the hardest of jigsaw puzzles. All his years of drawing and copying and assembling more ordinary skeletons had prepared him for this. He needed to recall every one of the two hundred and six bones in the body, and recognise their patterns, even on this miniature scale. His eyes throbbed; his fingers ached. He was going to raise a little girl from the dead, so the living might understand. With only bone and wire and glue he planned to make something that united – in the words of a recently dead poet of a medical persuasion – Beauty and Truth.

Her parents read of her death in the *Cork Inquirer*. Mr Crackham took the night ferry. In London he banged on doors of parish authorities and magistrates' courts, and toured the hospitals and morgues, but all the bodies he was shown were too big: 'This is not my daughter,' he repeated.

He never caught up with Dr Gilligan – who'd absconded from his lodgings owing £25 – but he did find his way in the end to Surgeons' Hall in Lincoln's Inn Fields. He got to the laboratory a week late. Dr Clift was putting the final touches to his masterpiece with a miniature screwdriver.

When the Irishman understood what he was looking at, he let out a roar that was not fully human. He tried to throw his arms around his Kitty, but something halted him.

This tinkling puppet was not his any more, if she had ever been. Her clean, translucent bones were strung as taut as pearls, and her spine was a metal rod. She stood on her tiny pedestal with her frilled knees together like a nervous dancer, about to curtsey to the world. Her ankles were delicately fettered; her thumbs were wired to the looped ribbons of her hips. Her palms tilted up as if to show she had nothing to hide.

Her head was a white egg, with eye holes like smudges made by a thumb. Nine teeth on the top row, nine on the bottom, crooked as orange pips. She grinned at the man who had been her father like a child at a party, with fear or excitement, he couldn't tell which.

How lovely she was.

*   *   *

168

It occurred to Dr Clift then, watching as the porters hauled the child's father off howling and kicking, that Kitty's bones would last longer than his own. She was a fossil, now; she had her niche in history. Shortly she would be placed on show in the Museum Hall between tanks that held a cock with a leg grafted on to its comb and a foetus with veins cast in red wax. She looked like a human house of cards, but nothing could knock her down. She would stand grinning at her baffled visitors until all those who'd ever known her were dust.

Note

The girl known as Caroline Crachami died on 3 June 1824, probably from a combination of TB and exhaustion. But basic facts about this child's nationality, age, medical history and life before arrival in England in 1823 are still disputed.

My inspiration and main source for 'A Short Story' was a long and highly original article by Gaby Wood, 'The Smallest of All Persons Mentioned in the Records of Littleness', published in the *London Review of Books*, 11 December 1997, and afterwards in volume form by Profile Books. I also drew on Richard Altick's *The Shows of London*. Crachami's skeleton, death mask, limb casts and accessories are displayed in the Hunterian Museum at the Royal College of Surgeons in Lincoln's Inn Fields, London, next to the remains of the giant, O'Brien.

Dido

I was in the Orangery at Kenwood that June morning, picking plums and grapes. I knew nothing. My name was Dido Bell.

The Orangery smelt of flowers and was warm, as ever; the underfloor was heated with pipes from the bakehouse next door. There were orange trees in tubs; they had never borne fruit yet, but my great-aunt and I had hopes for that summer. There were peach trees and myrtles and geraniums, sweet marjoram and lavender. I looked out the long windows, delighting as always in the prospect, the paths of grass and gravel that wound between the ivies and the cedars and the great beeches.

In the Hall, Diana ran along beside her nymphs and hounds; I traced her foot with my fingers. My great-aunt was in her China Closet, sorting her collection of Chenise, Derby, Worcester, Sèvres and Meissen, and not to be disturbed lest she drop something, the housekeeper said. I had nothing particular to occupy myself with that morning, having seen to the dairy and the poultry-yard already. My cousin Elizabeth was out on the terrace, having her portrait taken. A serene, sleepy air hung over the whole house.

My great-uncle was in his Library, peering at a letter, under the overmantel portrait of himself in his long tomato-red baronial robes with a bust of Homer. I tapped on the open door and asked if I should fetch my writing desk and take down his answer. Lord Mansfield looked over his spectacles a little distractedly and said no, not today.

'Have you been into the Cold Bath yet this morning, sir? The doctor said—'

'I'm perfectly well, Dido, don't fuss.'

I turned away, examined the carved letters on the bust by Nollekens. 'Remind me. *Uni Aequus Virtuti*?'

He smiled at me indulgently and looked up at his plaster self. 'Faithful to Virtue Alone,' he translated.

'Why did you pick that as a motto?'

'It means, my dear, that as Lord Chief Justice of England I must never allow personal considerations or whims to sway my judgement: I must follow pure principle. And now what I must do' – the frown creeping over him again – 'is finish reading this letter before I go in to the King's Bench.'

I thought my great-uncle might change his mind and ask me to take dictation after all – his eyes, like the rest of him, being nearly seventy years old – so I stood quietly in one of the Library's recesses. Beside his coffee tray lay a knot of rosebuds; Mr French the gardener always picked a nosegay on the summer days when the master had to drive into the stinking city. The Library was all blue and pink, sparkling with gold paint and red damask, and the air was still cool; the chill was delicious on my neck. I looked at the backs of the books, the orange and green and brown glow of their leathers; they would need another dusting soon. I contemplated the allegorical paintings above me. Justice reminded me of my great-uncle; Commerce, of my chickens, who were giving so many eggs this month that it was high time I sent some down to be sold in Hampstead. Navigation: that stood for my father, Rear Admiral John Lindsay of His Majesty's Navy. He had rescued my mother from captivity on a Spanish ship the year before I was born. I wrote him letters, telling him of my daily life at Kenwood with my cousin Elizabeth and our great-uncle and great-aunt, and sometimes when he was not too busy he dictated a reply.

The recess was lined with one of the great pier-glasses: seven and a half feet high, three and a half feet wide, the largest mirrors in England, or so Mr Chippendale assured my great-uncle. They had been brought from France by road and sea and road again, and not one of them had broken. The glass was not tarnished yet. It gave me back to myself: my hair was dressed very high and frizzy today, and my pointed face was the colour of boiling coffee.

'Dido, are you still here?' Great-Uncle Mansfield glanced up from his letter. 'I forgot to say, you're wanted on the terrace. I've told Zoffany to put you in Lady Elizabeth's portrait.'

I grinned at him and seized my basket; went into the Ante-Room, shutting the door softly behind me, stepped out the Venetian windows and on to the grass.

'What a charming property this is, Miss Dido, this ravishing villa of Kenwood,' murmured the painter with his foreign *r*s, as he arranged us. My cousin was to be seated on a rustic bench reading *Evelina*, catching my elbow as I rushed by – or pretended to, rather. 'Lay down your book, Lady Elizabeth, if you would be so very kind. Reach out and caress your cousin in passing,' he told her, 'to convey the warmth of familial friendship, but *regardez-moi, hein*? Eyes forward.'

Elizabeth was looking her usual loveliness in her new French pink *saque*, with her late mother's triple rope of pearls around her neck and rosebuds in her hair. I asked should I put on my patterned muslin, but Mr Zoffany said on the contrary, he had a special costume for me in his trunk. It was a fanciful thing in loose white satin, with a gauze shawl and an ostrich-feathered turban to match. When I came downstairs, transformed, he clipped

172

big gold earrings on to me; it was a most curious sensation. Catching sight of the basket of fresh-picked plums and grapes I had set down on the grass, he thrust it into my arms for a touch of the exotic, as he called it.

I stood as still as I could, in the frozen position he had put me in; I could not help but laugh at such theatricals. Elizabeth was just as bad; she kept her eyes forward in the correct pose, but she tickled my waist whenever the painter was not watching. Mr Zoffany was staring at me now, with a little frown. 'Miss Dido – if you would be so good as to touch your finger to your cheek just here – most becoming.' I obeyed. 'Exquisite,' he murmured. 'What contrasts!'

'Mr Adam, his Lordship's designer, you know, says variety is all,' I remarked.

'Very true, very picturesque,' said Mr Zoffany, his hands moving as fast as dragonflies.

'That's why he designed such a little vestibule leading to our Great Stairs,' I told him.

'Is it?' murmured Elizabeth, her eyes stealing to her novel.

'He once told me that the large goes with the small, the narrow demands the wide, the bright calls out for the sombre; beauty depends on contrast.'

Mr Zoffany suddenly smiled at me over his canvas, and beckoned me with one finger.

I ran to look over his shoulder at the preliminary marks on the canvas, and suddenly I saw what he meant. It was indeed a study in contrasts. Elizabeth was shown against a great dark bush – how her face and dress would glow like an angel when they were painted in – while my sketched figure stood up as black as the plums I was carrying, black against the pale sky in my white turban, with one black finger pointing to my black face as if to say, *look, look*.

173

I did not know what to say. But the painter, absorbed in his work again, was not asking my opinion, so I went back and stood in position. Elizabeth, peeking at the next page of *Evelina*, rested her hand on my elbow for support. Oddly restless, I looked past the little lakes of our estate, over the ripening fields, the land gently sloping south for miles down towards Greenwich Hospital and the famous cathedral of St Paul's. I often asked my great-aunt to take me into London, but she always said it was a wearisome place, and not healthful for a girl. If I narrowed my eyes I could just make out the Thames, speckled with traffic. I thought of my mother, who had been part of the cargo of a Spanish ship when my father had boarded it. My earlobes were beginning to ache under their weight of gold.

The housekeeper came out on the terrace to look for me. 'There's a visitor here for Lord Mansfield, Miss Dido; I keep telling the fellow the master's out, but he won't go.'

'I'll see to him.'

I ran up the Back Stairs to change out of my costume first. But when I stepped into the Hall in my blue polonaise ten minutes later, I stopped short. The stranger was gazing up at the portraits of my great-aunt's ancestors. He was tall, with an unfashionably long, shabby waistcoat, and carried a file of papers. I had never seen a black man before, except in books.

He looked startled to see me too; he bowed a little warily. 'Good day, Miss.' He had a strange accent; like some of my great-uncle's American visitors, but different. 'Would you be Lady Mansfield's . . . maid?'

'No,' I said a little sharply, 'her great-niece.'

His eyes bulged white at that. 'I understand Lord Mansfield is not at home?'

'That's so.'

'I sent him a letter, Miss, ma'am, I mean' – he stepped forward,

174

as if to reduce the distance between us, and his face loosened into dark lines – 'a letter of great importance, at least to me, and I was wondering if he had received it safely.'

'I do not know,' I said. His hand was pink underneath, just like mine; I wanted to touch it.

'His Lordship must receive many letters,' the man said hoarsely, and swallowed, 'but I very much hope – it is of the greatest urgency, not just to me but to thousands of others – that he read it.'

'I will be sure to pass on your message on his Lordship's return,' I said, too stiffly.

He was turning away when I asked for his name. 'I beg your pardon. Somerset,' he said, and repeated it doggedly; 'my name is Somerset.'

After the stranger was gone I stood still for a moment, in the Hall. When I drifted into my great-uncle's Library, the letter he had been reading was still open on the desk, with the rosebuds forgotten and wilting beside it. I thought I would just check the name on the bottom, to see if it said Somerset; then if the man came back, later that day, I would be able to tell him that his letter had been received and read, at least.

My eyes strayed up to the top of the page.

shackles and whipped me like a dog till the skin of my back was in ribbons. When after many years in England I ran away from this devilish master he had me kidnapped and pressed on a ship in the Thames wh was bound for Jamaica. Kind friends secured my release but now my so-called master demands me back and I live every day in peril. The matter is in your hands Lord Mansfield sir. I hear that you have on sevl prior occasions ruled that blacks should be returned for resale in

175

*the Indies out of respect for the law of property. I ask
you now your Lordship if I may be so bold to respect the
law of humanity instead.*

Your servant (tho no man's slave),
James Somerset

I dropped the page as if it was on fire. I was shaking all over.
I had known that such things happened; I must have known.
But I never had cause to think about them, in the course of a
day at Kenwood. If I dwelt on such things at all, I supposed
they happened far away, to unimaginable people who were used
to such things, people for whom nothing could be done. Not
here in England. Not to somebody like James Somerset. Like
me.

I folded the letter up small and put it in my dress. Faintly I
heard my name being called in the Ante-Room. 'Dido! Dido!'
Not a real name, of course, but a play one. I had been baptised
Elizabeth, but when my cousin Elizabeth came to live at
Kenwood, I became Dido – nicknamed for an African queen, I
was told, who was once abandoned on a shore.

'I must go out, Elizabeth,' I told my pink-cheeked cousin as
I brushed past her in the Hall.

'Out?' she repeated, disconcerted. 'Out where, Dido? For a
walk?'

'An urgent message has come for his Lordship. I shall need
the carriage –'

'But he's taken the carriage into town himself, silly.'

Of course he had. 'Then' – my heart pounding as if I was
running a race – 'I shall tell John to saddle the old roan to the
little curricle.'

'But Dido, dear—'

'I tell you, it can't wait.'

176

I ran upstairs to fetch my shawl, before she could stop me. I had never behaved like this in my life. I was Dido Bell, known to the family and visitors as a sometimes pert but amiable girl. What was I doing? Was I a fool, or had I been a fool all my life till today? The walls of my room were covered in China papers; little people in strange draperies and pointed hats walked up and down. I remembered Mr Adam telling me that Chinese figures were best for bedchambers, as they were conducive to dreaming. But I was not dreaming now.

Out in the coach house, I overrode John's protests; I looked him square in the eye and told him that his Lordship had made me swear to bring him any message received today. In a quarter of an hour, the curricle was wheeling out the front gate and heading straight for the City.

The journey was a short one; it all went by me in a blur of stink and noise. I did not even know we had reached the Inner Temple till John pointed at the gate with his whip. As he was helping me jump down, a passing girl squealed 'Look at that dirty blackamoor got up like a lady!'

Shock stopped my breath. I had never been spoken to that way in my life. My heart was stuck in my throat like a piece of gristle. What was I, I asked myself now? Blackamoor or lady? A terrible mixture. Neither fish nor flesh nor fowl.

I asked John to escort me in, but he set his jaw and said he had to stay with the horse and curricle or they would be stolen in a blink. So I marched in the gate myself. Pale men and red-faced ones pushed past me in long robes; I avoided their stares. My great-uncle's chambers were on King's Bench Walk, I knew that much. At the top of the steps I cleared my throat and asked to see Lord Mansfield. The porter did not hear me the first time, so I had to repeat myself.

He stared back with hostility. 'About the Somerset case, is it?

There's been dozens of you here already this week, plaguing his Lordship. I could report you for trying to pervert the course of justice, so I could. Who's your master?'

'I have none,' I said through my teeth.

'Runaway rabbit, are you, then?' he said with a dirty grin. 'Who's paying for those fine frills?' He pulled at my polonaise.

I could not bear to explain myself to him. 'Kindly let me in. Lord Mansfield will wish to see me at once.'

'That's what they all say, sweetheart!' But the porter stood back just enough to let me squeeze past him.

In the warren of chambers, I had to ask my way three times. I was on the verge of tears when I burst into my great-uncle's office at last.

'Dido?' He looked up, appalled.

The younger gentleman beside him looked me up and down in amusement. 'I didn't know you'd any yourself, Mansfield.'

There was a silence; I waited, sucking on my lip. Finally my great-uncle said, 'Miss Bell is a close relation.'

'Relation?' repeated his colleague. Then, 'Pardon me, I'm sure,' and he sauntered out of the room.

When we were alone I saw how angry my great-uncle was; there were red spots high on his wrinkled cheeks. 'Why do you disturb me here?'

I wanted to burst into tears. Instead I stepped up to him and pulled Somerset's letter out of my bosom. I waited to be sure he recognised it, and then I said, 'Am I your property, sir?'

'No, Dido. What nonsense. You're—'

'Am I your great-niece, just as Elizabeth is?' I cut in.

'Of course,' he said, bewildered.

'Do you love me like her?'

'Rather more, if the truth be told,' he said through his teeth.

This startled me a little. I sat down in a velvet chair, without

178

being asked. After a minute, I said 'The porter seemed to think I was your slave.'

'Well, he was mistaken.'

I lifted my chin. 'How are people to know I'm free, if my skin says otherwise?'

My great-uncle struggled for words. He opened his hands, at last. 'It's an imperfect world. What would you have of me, Dido?'

He meant it rhetorically, I knew, but all of a sudden I felt like the girl in the fairy-tale, who demanded three wishes. 'The first thing I want,' I improvised, 'is a piece of paper stating that I am a free person.'

He shrugged. 'Certainly. But there's no need—'

'No need? What if you're not here, next time? What if the porter decides to presume that I've stolen your chaise, stolen this dress, even?' I plucked at my skirts. 'What if I end up in gaol or on a ship in the Thames, seized as *lost property*?'

'I'll do it, then. I'll write a declaration of your freedom this minute,' his Lordship said crossly, reaching for a pen.

'And I want a salary,' I added.

His brow creased. 'What fit of sulks is this, Dido? You're one of the family.'

'Am I, though? Am I not the dairy-maid, and the poultry-keeper?'

He sighed. 'Your position at Kenwood—'

'When you have guests,' I interrupted him, 'I'm not asked in till dinner's over.'

My great-uncle squirmed. 'Why, you know what guests can be like. The English are famed for their prejudice against foreigners. Why I myself, for instance, as a Scot—'

'I was born in England,' I interrupted him.

'Well, Dido,' he said miserably, 'you must come in to dinner in future. Truly, I never knew you minded.'

179

'I didn't, till today,' I said. 'Till I knew what it meant. Now I see why you've kept me hidden away at Kenwood.'

'The country air is much more wholesome for you, and for all my family,' he insisted, putting his hand over mine.

His skin was as soft as chicken feathers, and spotted with age; I pulled away. 'Did you take me in as an unpaid companion for Lady Elizabeth, was that it?' I asked, searching his face. 'One little motherless girl to amuse the other. A black face in the painting, as a foil for the white!'

'You are most precious to your cousin, to us all,' he said, his throat working. 'I thought you understood that.'

I steeled myself against him. 'What about my salary?'

'It's not money I grudge you, my dear,' he said painfully; 'don't I often give you presents in silver? But a salary – that has such a cold ring to it.'

'Call it a quarterly allowance, then,' I said.

He sighed heavily and began sharpening his pen.

A third wish, I thought, there has to be a third. And then I remembered what began it all. 'One last thing. James Somerset,' I said. 'Let him go.'

'Ah, now, my dear,' said my great-uncle grimly, 'that's a complicated matter.'

'Don't I know it?'

'You meddle in what doesn't concern you.'

Rage, like ink spilled across my eyes. 'Whom does it concern more than me,' I shouted, 'whose mother was a slave, your nephew's slave and whore? I wonder, did he free her before she died? Did he take the shackles off when she was giving birth to me?' Now I did not care if I could be heard all through the Inner Temple. 'Whom should such matters *concern* more than me, your little dusky plaything?'

Lord Mansfield bent across the desk and seized me, then,

enclosed me in his arms. I could smell the dust and sourness of his old robes. 'Dido,' he sobbed, 'Dido Bell, my sweet girl, how can you say such things?'

I rested in his embrace for a few seconds, then pulled away. 'Let James Somerset go free.'

'But don't you see, my dear,' he said, straightening his spectacles with one shaky hand, 'I mustn't be swayed by personal loyalties. *Faithful to Virtue Alone*, don't you know.'

'What virtue has a man with no loyalties?'

He winced. 'But I have many. The very fact that I am known to have in my family – to be bound by every tender tie, to, to—'

'A mulatto.'

'To *you*, Dido, makes it all the more imperative that I should be seen to maintain objectivity in this most controversial case.'

'I'm not asking a favour for myself,' I told him coldly. 'I ask justice for Somerset.'

The old man breathed heavily. Finally he said, 'I have always called American slavery an odious institution.'

I waited.

'But the fact is, its effects are woven through our whole social fabric. To rule that a master mayn't put his own slave on a ship – well, it could bring on ruin.'

'For whom?'

'For everyone, Dido. Agriculture, trade, the economies of many nations . . . the consequences . . . if misunderstood, if too widely interpreted,' he said, almost babbling, seizing my hand, 'such a ruling could lead to fifteen thousand slaves casting off their yokes in the morning! If no man may own and control another in England, some will argue, how may he do so elsewhere?'

I felt power like sugar in my mouth.

'At the end of an honourable career, Dido,' the old judge said, clinging to my fingers, 'I might stand accused of having brought down chaos on us all.'

'Should I take my leave, then?' I asked him, at the end of a long silence. 'Is it time for us to part?'

His mouth moved, but he could not speak.

'Are we not family, then, after all?'

He wept. He nodded. He called for the carriage to take us home.

Note

Dido Bell, aka Dido Elizabeth Belle, aka Elizabeth Dido Lindsay, was born in England to an African slave woman who had been on a Spanish ship captured by Sir John Lindsay (one of Lord Mansfield's nephews) in the West Indies.

My sources for 'Dido' include the diary of Thomas Hutchinson (published 1886), who visited Kenwood on 29 August 1779. Zoffany's portrait of Dido and Lady Elizabeth Murray hangs in Scone Palace. I found much conflicting information on her in Gretchen Gerzina, *Black England*; James Shyllon, *Black Slaves in Britain*; Julius Bryant, *The Iveagh Bequest, Kenwood*; and Gene Adams, 'Dido Elizabeth Belle: A Black Girl at Kenwood', *Camden History Review* 12 (1984).

On 22 June 1772 Lord Mansfield finally delivered what became known as the Somerset Ruling, which said that no master was to be allowed to take a slave abroad by force. Many abolitionists interpreted it broadly to mean that slavery was now illegal in Britain, and thousands of slaves left their masters or demanded wages. But black people continued to be bought, sold, hunted and kidnapped in England, and were sometimes shipped back to the West Indies, for many decades to come. It is not clear what age Dido was in 1772, or whether she had any influence on Mansfield's decision, but Thomas Hutchinson quoted a Jamaican planter who said of Somerset, 'He will be set free, for Lord Mansfield keeps a Black in his house which governs him and the whole family.'

Lindsay and Mansfield both left Dido substantial sums of money, and Mansfield took the precaution of confirming in his will that she was free. After his death she left Kenwood and probably married a Frenchman, because in 1794 she was listed in the family accounts at Hoare's Bank as Mrs Dido Elizabeth Davinier.

The Necessity of Burning

Adrift in a boat made of butter on a sweet milk sea, she glimpses a castle on the horizon, a stately palace built of cheese and ornamented with curds of whey . . .

Margery Starre wakes from a dream of fat. Her mouth is as dry as a sack. Late afternoon sun prises the shutters apart.

For the first time in her forty-seven years it occurs to her not to get up. June fifteenth, a Saturday, a working day like any other and the Widow Starre was only having half an hour's shut-eye but now she's inclined to press her face back into her mattress and wait for the old straw to tickle her back to sleep. Let her neighbours on Bridge Street think she's fallen sick; let the Cam flow green and sluggish below her window; let this day, out of the too many days she has laboured through on this earth, wind into evening without her.

She scratches a bite on her hip. No, it's not straw she can smell, it's trouble. There's been whispering at corners and proclamations against unlawful assemblies. The peasants' army has crossed the Thames, or so they say. Kent's risen against the poll tax, and Essex too; Bury St Edmunds, St Albans, and Norwich, even. Trouble's on its way across the Fens like a flood of brine. She can hear it coming now outside her window in the hiss of

184

geese being driven across the Bridge after market, and the wooden soles of the goose maid, in the clop of a horse and the complaining wheels of the cart it pulls, in the banging of Ned Smith's hammer three houses up the hill, in the mewing of the new baby two floors above the room where Margery Starre lies, face down, wishing this long afternoon over. Trouble has got into her own head, too. There's a treasonous rhyme going round, she picked it up this morning in the market where she was buying a pig's trotter for her dinner:

> *When Adam delved and Eve span,*
> *Who was then the gentleman?*

But she gets up and goes about the last business of the day, of course. The Widow Starre wouldn't have lasted forty-seven years and outlived most of the people she's ever known if she was in the habit of forgetting her business and opening her door to trouble.

Five o'clock. She sips the ale and lets it linger on her tongue; faintly sour, or is her mouth still full of sleep? For supper she eats old cheese and onions off a trencher of dark stale bread. Licking her knife clean, she puts it back into the sheath that hangs from her girdle.

Then Margery goes into the back room. Edgy, she checks everything twice. She rakes her fingers through the barley, oats, wheat and malt, looking out for weevils or worms, peering into the barrels in the angular light. She sniffs at the pungent mash vat, checks the coolers and the rudders and the great copper kettle that's big enough for a woman to climb in and lie down. She's promised this batch of ale to the owner of the Pig and Parrot for Wednesday; a halfpenny a gallon she'll get for it.

In her time, Margery Starre has made hay and cheese, built

walls and tended pigs. Back home in her village she used to run a tavern out of her own kitchen, but she wouldn't try that in this town. Such troublemakers as the scholars are, with their pointed shoes and their high laughter. They'll swap jokes in Latin and Greek all night, then throw the trestles in the river. The worst of it is, you can't say a thing against them because they're under the protection of the University. Town hates gown, and no wonder.

It's not the King's Sheriff but the University's Chancellor who's the real master in this town. It's he who has whores arrested if they pick up scholar boys, and fines bakers for selling a loaf that's half an ounce too light. The University holds all liberties, all the privileges granted it by a long line of kings; it oversees the weights and measures, the selling of bread and meat and fish and wine and ale; it holds governance and punishment of all things. Last year, a brewstress from Castle Street was found guilty of selling weakened ale to the scholars. In Margery's village you'd be fined sixpence for that, if anything, but the woman shouted out in court that her accusers were a pack of liars, and Chancellor said it was high time to set an example to these grasping townsfolk. He had her ducked at the Stool by the Bridge, not five yards from this house. The woman survived, but took a spluttering cough that killed her by Christmas. Margery passes the Stool every day; she tries not to look into the water, or imagine the press of it in her lungs, the brief green taste of death. It reminds her of one of the rules she holds to: *Never cross a cleric*.

But what do they do all day, you may ask, these scholars and their masters who lord it over those who feed and clothe them? What's their honest work, their valuable trade? Books, that's all! It makes Margery laugh. These clerics spend all day reading books and copying them out on to paper, and what's that but dried mash of dirty old rags or straw? Some books are the size of your palm, others the width of your table, all with leather covers as hard as wood. Some are psalters and some are hour-books and some are romances and Margery's damned if she knows the difference. In her youth, at least a man who was reading muttered the words aloud, but this sinister new fashion for reading with eyes alone means a bystander can't even tell if it's scripture or fable! All Margery knows is, this strange town is built on paper, and it prizes greasy old books above wool or wine or roasted goose.

What good ever came out of a book, she wonders sometimes? She doesn't need to read them to know what's in them; she's heard enough. Tales of lickerous widows who force men to lie with them; tales of clever young men who trick girls into lying with them; whole books full of wicked wives, like Eve who let the snake into Paradise. No wonder, Margery reckons, seeing as it's men who write the books.

Now she comes to think of it, there's an anchoress down at Norwich who lives bricked up in a cellar and has visions and has set them down in a book. Sometimes, this woman claims, the devil comes and seizes her by the throat with his big stinking paws. So that's where book-learning gets you!

No, Margery Starre is better off keeping to herself and making her ale. Brewing has always been women's business, and folk will always want the stuff, that's one sure thing. No one can live without ale, whatever may happen; whatever may overtake the land. Ale for bridals and wakes, for dinner and breakfast, for thirst and misery, in times of merriment and disaster alike.

But trouble hangs like mould on the air: she can smell it. Where will the ruckus begin, when it begins, as surely it must? On Peas Hill or Findsilver Lane or Butchers Row, among the clinking weights at the Tolbooth, in the gutters of Foul Lane under the college privies? In St Rhadegund's Convent, where the dozen remaining nuns sing like swans and nibble their crusts to make them last? In the stew run by the Weavers Guild, where the whores lie counting the cracks in the ceiling? Between the pursed mouths of the fish caught in the tangled river, in the taut bowstrings of the archers always practising on the Green?

Margery Starre jumps at the sound of a bell. Then another, louder. That must be St Benet's, calling the boys to their last lesson of the day. Margery looked in the door of St Benet's once, as she was passing with a great jar of honey on her head. The scholars knelt there on rushes, taking words down on green wax tablets – puny half-sized lads, some of them – while the Master read aloud in Latin from a long scroll unwinding from a wooden pin like a distaff. Vellum, that was, Margery knows that much; the skin of a new-born kid or lamb, stretched and polished thin till you'd never know it was hide. Some books are made of vellum instead of paper, stiff buckled sheets of it gone dark at the edges from handling, with little pictures in blue and scarlet and gold. Not that she saw any pictures that day, because the Master saw her looking in, and he barked a word at one of the boys, who ran and shut the door in her face. It's odd, she thinks now, that a woman can sell a field or pay a fine as well as any man, but she can't walk in the door of a college without spreading havoc.

No, those aren't Benet's bells, she realises; they're lower. Besides, she's seen no young scholars out this evening, and there's another sign of trouble. Most Saturdays they're to be found hanging round Fitzbilly's pie shop, with their catapults and scornful looks. The older ones roam the streets in packs of three score or more, and nobody can bar their way. Scholars will never be towns-folk; they're only here to study their seven arts for seven years, serving their time before they go out into the world as priests or physicians, lawyers or treasurers. To them, this town is no more than an inn on their road.

Could these be the bells of Great St Mary's she's hearing? But those never toll except for Sunday Mass. Besides, they've gone on too long. And now Margery lets herself listen, there are feet thudding by as fast as goats, and the odd shout on the warm evening air.

The Widow Starre stands in her doorway, hands braced against the jamb. It's started, then. The bells of Great St Mary's must be the signal. Her heart joins in, clanging against her ribs. Cambridge is rising.

'Our time is come!'

Midnight on Saturday, and the old rabble-rouser howls out his message from where he stands on the keystone of the bridge. His beard is white and stringy.

'Ye are folk in bondage as were the Israelites in Egypt of old. And now comes this new poll tax, this cruel stone laid on the head of every person in England, which to the rich man is felt as a mere pebble, but as for the bondsman, it weighs him down and bends his neck. This is too much to bear!'

Behind her barred shutters, the Widow Starre covers her eyes and tries not to listen.

'All men be made equal in the beginning, come of one father Adam and one mother Eve,' roars the rabble-rouser almost joyfully, 'whereby then can these gentlemen say they be greater than we? No more will the honest folk of Cambridge squirm under the boot of this University! No more shall ye sweat your days to pay these foul taxes to the King's cruel ministers! For too long,' he bawls, his voice cracking, 'these lords and bishops and clerics have gone clad in camlet and ermine, while ye wear but coarse cloth. For too long have they feasted on wine and spices and white bread, while ye be choking on rye and husks and plain water!'

Margery sits in the dark. She blew out her lantern hours ago,

189

for fear to be noticed. There's not much *plain water* getting drunk tonight. She can hear the shrieks and splashes of men fighting in the river. The Mayor has issued a Proclamation of Revolt, or so they say. The College of Corpus Christi – landlord to half the town, including Margery – has been sacked. Not an hour ago, she saw three girls stagger up the street, bearing between them an oak door with the College's crest on it. Margery felt a tiny flicker of excitement at that news, but still, it's a dreadful thing, and one of the mob lies dead of his wounds, and in time, she's sure, the tenants will all pay for the damage ten times over in higher rents. Also a tax collector's son is holed up in the little church of St Giles, claiming sanctuary from the mob who tried to cut his head off in the graveyard. Rebellion passes from street to street like a burning sickness, like a plague, like the Black Death that ate through England the year Margery turned twelve. Terrible!

She's done nothing, and no one will be able to say she has, afterwards. She's stayed home and waited for it all to be over. Do her neighbours not know what happens to rebels and rioters, to all who spit in the face of the King's law or the Church's? What kinds of fools are they, that they'd bring down ruin on themselves?

'Servitude to lord or cleric be against the will of God,' bawls the rabble-rouser, 'for why else would he have made us all the same on the first naked day, formed of the same dust? So throw down this yoke, men of Cambridge, and seize your liberty!'

Back in her village, Margery was a bondswoman, like half her neighbours, and never thought to feel any shame about it. She worked two days a week for the lord and paid all her taxes, whether to the lord or the priest: she paid the plough-alms and the church-tithe and the tallage, the merchet when she married Roger Starre, and the soul-scot when their child died, and again the best cow as a death-duty when Roger was taken too, by a gripping of the bowels, and then the chevage fine for leaving the estate, the day she set off for Cambridge. She paid all her dues and didn't give any trouble.

She's never regretted moving to the big town, though. Once she'd lived here, breathing free air, for a year and a day, she knew she was a bondswoman no more. There are still taxes to pay, but she works for no master but herself. This is a better life for a widow; she has fresh rushes on the floor, two windows with shutters on them and a hearth of stone. She eats barley bread instead of pottage; she's better off than she ever expected to be. Why would she be ungrateful? Why would she risk losing all she's won for herself over the years?

The rabble-rouser is waving a torch now, scattering sparks in the hot night. 'Men and women of Cambridge, your grievances are sore! Who is this puffed-up Chancellor, that ye should pay him a fee or a fine for every step ye take? The same man who forbids all tournaments and frolicks for five miles around the town, in case the noise might cause nuisance to his scholars at their book-reading! Tell me, who are these masters and scholars, these lily-handed churchmen and bookmen who never worked a day in their lives?'

It's no good defying them, Margery could tell this stranger. Question a cleric, and he'll find laws and precedents enough in his books to make a fool of you. Attack one and his whole band of brothers-in-the-cloth will back him. In Margery's village, in her mother's time, there was a girl who was found to have falsely charged a rape against the priest, and the church court set her a dreadful penance, that she was to walk barefoot to Rome and back again. She set off all right – the whole village watched her go – but she never came back, Margery remembers.

'Widow Starre!' It's her neighbour, Philbert Carrier, from

191

across the way, gone sixty years old. His tunic is all askew. 'Come down to Market Square. The bonfire's started!'

She sees the red smudge of his cheeks close up between the slats of her shutters.

'Come now.'

'You're looters and rioters and fools,' she tells him in an unsteady voice. 'Are you not afraid of the Sheriff's men?'

His grin is wide and toothless. 'They can't clap us *all* in the gaol, can they? It wouldn't hold a tenth of the town!'

And with that he's gone, stumbling across the bridge with the rest of them.

A little later comes the sound of men's feet stamping in time to the rhyme they shout out:

> *Those who can't eat will meet.*
> *Those who can't make will break.*
> *Those who can't read will lead.*
> *Those who can't write will fight.*

Margery doesn't go to her bed. She sits bent over on her stool, almost dozing sometimes until she jerks awake with a little choking sound. She holds her eyes shut and waits for the night to be over.

The Widow Starre wakes in a silent town. She puts her head out her door on to Bridge Street, and it's as if all the townsfolk have run away in the night. She crumbles an oat cake in ale for breakfast but can't make herself swallow it.

She knows she's safer in than out, but she can't bear to stay at home any longer. The bridge is half-smashed; she has to edge along the rim of it, testing each board with her foot. Below her the weed-choked river smells of ferment. Something drifts by,

192

and she thinks it's a body, till she recognises it as a child's coat.

She walks warily through town, past St Clement's and the round church of Holy Sepulchre, past All Saints and St Michael's. The streets are deserted, littered with old vegetables and the odd shattered pane of glass. She goes round the long way to avoid Market Square, in case of a mob. At the edge of Petty Curie a huge cart lies on its side, its wheels askew. Under it two men lie in a tangle; not dead, she sees, just drunk and snoring. Does this mean it's all over? Or are they only resting before the next bout?

She hasn't heard the bells of Great St Mary's this morning, but when she reaches the church she hears the mumble of the rector saying Mass, as on any other Sunday, so she goes in and finds herself a place to stand at the back, behind the scholars' benches. Because this is what she's always done; because she can't think of anything else to do today.

She doesn't understand the Latin but she knows which bits to stand or kneel for. The congregation is small and subdued, dark around the eyes. Margery should have had her breakfast. When she feels a little weak, she squats down on the muddy stone floor. Her eyes rest on the altar cloths and the canopy and the holy cruets and the statue of the Virgin and the stone font with the wooden lid that's locked to keep the holy water safe from witches.

For the sermon, the pale-faced rector switches to English. He walks down the church and climbs the stairs to the pulpit. The people wait to hear the Scripture theme announced, but instead the rector knots his hands and speaks without preamble. 'Today is Whitsunday, the feast of Pentecost,' he begins in his quiet educated voice, 'when Our Lord's Apostles in the upper room were blessed with tongues of fire. But last night in this town a fire came down which was not a holy fire, but rather a sinful fire, a fire of rebellion and black treason.'

Margery Starre stares up at him, her mouth dry. Not a sound from the congregation except the occasional cough.

'Men of this town have talked of grievances and deservings,' the rector comments, only a little louder. 'But I say to you, when and by whom were you told that you *deserve* anything? Everything you receive in this life is in God's gift, and if others receive more than you, that is by God's will. We men of the cloth, we men of the book,' he added, standing a little straighter in his bright robes, 'have been placed over you by virtue of our greater wisdom. Whoever raises his hand against one of us is damned. I promise you all, whoever takes any part in this foul rebellion will go to Hell.' He still speaks gracefully, as a poet might. 'People of Cambridge, do you recall what you have been taught of Hell?'

Margery turns her head to look for a way out, but the floor is covered with kneeling bodies.

'Because light is reserved for God's chosen ones, Hell is the place of darkness, which rings always with the horrid roaring of blackened devils.'

All at once she remembers what she never lets herself remember, the birth of her son.

'Because coolness is the reward of a clean spirit, in Hell there is eternally the necessity of burning.'

He came out from her legs like a skinny little eel, past midnight. She was only twenty-three, young Goodwife Starre, but she knew enough to be afraid: this one didn't cry like proper babies cry. She bawled for her husband to send for the village priest to christen him quick. An hour passed, and the priest still wasn't come down. His wife (concubine, some called her) sent a message to say he was drunk and couldn't be woken.

'It is the place of weeping, and the gnashing of teeth, the crying of *Woe, woe!*'

How clearly Margery remembers, half a lifetime later, when

she's forgotten so much else. The midwife wailed; she said she'd christen the child herself if she only knew the words. So Margery shouted for a basin of clean water and her husband brought it in. The tiny boy was sticky now, marked with his blood and the prints of her hands. Knowing no Latin, Margery said it in English, all in a rush, as she dipped his whole head into the water: '*I christen thee both flesh and bone in the name of the Son and the Father and the Holy Ghost.*'

And then her son cried, a proper lusty cry, and she put him to her nipple and he sucked, and all was well.

Faintly she can hear the rector of St Mary's now, still calm-voiced, reading from a big book open on the lectern in front of him. 'The necessity of burning means that if anyone in Hell asks for butter, he receives only brimstone; if he would give a thousand pounds for a cup of water, he shall have none. There shall be flies that bite his flesh, and his clothing shall be worms. God cannot be merciful, because his mercy is saved for the deserving.'

But Margery won't listen. Her mind runs back to the night she gave suck to her son, and how she let herself doze at last, how she couldn't help it. And in the morning he was cool on her belly, chilly as a small bag of barley.

Then the village priest came down to her cottage, his eyes lidded against the headache.

'Father,' she told him, 'you should have brought the lantern and bell. What this child needs is burial.'

'Hold on,' he told her hoarsely. 'Did you christen him yourself, is that what I hear?'

'That's right, she did,' muttered Rogar Starre, almost proudly.

'What did you say, exactly?' the priest asked Margery.

'I said the words,' she repeated, confused.

'Which words?'

She wept then, as she said them again, over the tiny creature who was dead at the foot of the bed: '*I christen thee both flesh and bone in the name of the Son and the Father and the Holy Ghost.*'

The priest was shaking his head. 'Ah, woman,' he said crossly.

'What?'

'What is it?' asked Roger.

Margery was almost shrieking. 'What? Aren't those the right words?'

'Aye,' the priest said, pursing his lips, 'but in the wrong order. The Father goes before the Son, as any ignoramus knows. It's *the name of the Father and the Son and the Holy Ghost.*'

She stared at him. 'What does that mean?'

'It means this child's soul is lost to hellfire through your carelessness, woman, that's what it means!'

She said nothing, then. She didn't go for the man's throat; she didn't cry, even. She and Roger stared at each other, and the priest walked home to his wife. The next day the nameless child was buried – not in holy ground in the churchyard, but down by the stream, in a hollow his father dug him, no bigger than a rabbit hole. Margery used to wonder, after that, if Roger Starre blamed her for consigning his son's tiny soul to the flames, but she never found a way to ask him, in the few years before he died himself.

A terrible pounding. When the Widow Starre comes back to the present, kneeling in Great St Mary's church, where the rector is still explaining the horrors of hellfire, she realizes that nobody is listening to him any more. All heads are turned to the back of the church, where the barred doors are shaking like the skin of a drum. A crash, at last, and they splinter open.

The rector pauses, mid-sentence. His slim finger marks the word where he stopped reading.

The rebels race up the aisle, and the congregation shrinks back. Somebody – Philbert Carrier, in an incongruous yellow velvet cap – hauls the book off the lectern.

'How dare you!' The rector's voice has cracked at last. 'This book has been in the possession of the Holy Church for three hundred years.'

'High time it went on the bonfire, then,' says Philbert Carrier easily, tucking it under his arm.

Margery Starre feels a huge gulp of laughter in her throat.

After that it all moves very quickly. Most of the Mass-goers slip out the door, but Margery stays where she is, crouched on the stone floor, fascinated. The rebels shove the rector into the back room and come back staggering under the weight of an enormous chest filled with jewelled chalices, silver plate, but also rolls upon rolls of yellowed papers.

'Widow Starre!' Philbert Carrier sings out her name as soon as he catches sight of her. 'Do you know what we've got here?'

She gets to her feet, stiff-jointed.

'The charters!' he roars. 'Every liberty and privilege of the University is writ down on these scrolls and sealed with royal wax. How fast do you think they'll burn, Margery?'

He's never called her that before. She answers before she's had time to think; 'Not fast enough,' she says, and runs to help the men drag the chest out into the daylight.

In Market Square the bonfire rages against the pale Sunday morning sky. Doors, windows, posts and rafters frame its scarlet heart. The heat is fierce; it draws Margery Starre like a child.

A bearded man tosses some writing tablets onto the pyre, and the green wax runs off like Cam water. A book flies past Margery through the sooty air, like a heavy bird briefly lifted on stiff leather wings, and lands with a terrible scattering of papers. They singe, their edges curl up prettily like the thinnest pastry. They dance as

197

if glad to have the words cleaned off them in this purgatorial fire.

Yes, Margery Starre thinks, let the old lying books be cast into the fire like gnawed bones with no juice nor marrow left in them, like skeletons that are good for nothing else. She dwells for a moment on the years, the lives of scritch-scratching work spent on these flaring pages. Well, let the learned churchmen see now how little their labours have amounted to in the end: no more than all the ale she ever brewed or the milk she ever had in her to give, gone now, dried up in the blaze of this morning.

Margery Starre wades into the crowd, hoists a book about the weight of her son on the night he was born and died, tosses it into the bluest tongue of the flames. She snatches an armful of scrolls from a cobbler's wife and slings them one by one into the crackling bonfire. The pen outdoes the sword, or so they say, but Margery reckons the flame outdoes them both.

Of course there'll be punishment. Is there a single day that doesn't drag its punishment behind it, as a ewe her filthy tail? Margery knows and right now Margery couldn't give a fart. Once in a while, comes a day unlike all the others, priceless in your hand like a peppercorn you must wager the rest of your days to win.

The flames lick lovingly. The scent of black soot clouds round Margery Starre. It's the sweetest smell she can remember. She goes closer, breathing destruction, and dips her hands into the delicate ash. She feels no pain. Her palms are singeing. She scatters the ash on the air like rice at a wedding, like blossom at the end of spring. 'Away with the learning of the clerics!' she bawls, hoarse with laughter; 'away with it!'

And even though she knows there are hundreds of books still locked up safe in the libraries and universities of the world, still the churchmen will tremble when they hear of Margery Starre – read of her, even, maybe. In the turning of a page, in the lifting of a pen, in the taking of a breath, they will pause to think how fast paper burns.

Note

When the Peasants' Revolt came to the city of Cambridge on 15 June 1381, and University charters and books were burnt in Market Square, an old woman called Margery Starre is said to have scattered the ashes and shouted 'Away with the learning of the clerks, away with it.' This brief anecdote, the basis for 'The Necessity of Burning', is found in the Arundel MSS.350 fol 15.b (British Library), first translated and published in *Victoria History of the County of Cambridgeshire*, Vol. III (1948). My source for detailed information on the Revolt was Rowland Parker, *Town and Gown: The 700 Years' War in Cambridge* (1983).

The violence in Cambridge was quelled by the Bishop of Ely four days after it began, and all the University's privileges were restored. Margery Starre is not one of the rioters recorded as having been imprisoned or executed, and nothing further is known of her.

Looking for Petronilla

I've been away too long.

The plane took me from London to Dublin in less than an hour. I would have come this way before if I had known how simple it was. When I first took the boat to England, vomiting up my whole self into the Irish Sea, I swore I'd never go back. But most promises wear out in the end. This plane trip was almost merry, clouds back-lit by champagne.

I bought it in honour of Petronilla. Since she couldn't be here today it seemed only fitting to toast her virtues in overpriced bubbly, ten thousand feet above the island she never left.

The rented Volvo took me to Kilkenny with surprising speed. They've built craft shops on every corner, and knocked down a lot of old houses. Kyteler's Inn is still there, though; its wooden lines stand firm against the swarm of tourists. There's an Alice's Restaurant in the cellars ('It's a kind of magic!' jokes the sign, catching the sunlight), and upstairs is called Nero's; how very suitable. What's your poison, traveller?

I stand at the bar and order a glass of the best red they have. I look around, waiting for the centuries to fall away, but my eyes lodge on the chintzy little tablecloths and chairs. I am so used to the twentieth century that it is almost impossible to imagine myself back to the fourteenth. Hard to believe that this round-bellied building was ever cold and damp, with one fire sighing and the smell of tallow flaring in the nostrils of visitors.

I peer at the wall, where a Disney hag pours cups of smoking brew for four little men with uneasy expressions. Perhaps they have noticed that their shoes, toes tied to their knees, are from the wrong country and century. I read through the five-line caption, which is a tribute to the powers of invention. Nothing worth losing my temper over. Why should anyone remember, anyway, except someone like me whose business it is? There's been a lot of water under the bridge since 1324. History always becomes a cartoon, where it survives at all. Your best hope for a ride towards posterity is the bandwagon of folklore.

'Oldest house in Kilkenny, this is.'

I accept the wineglass from the greying woman behind the bar. 'So they say.'

'You know the story?'

'Oh yes.' I take a sip: not dry enough. I wonder what kind of hash this woman could make of the tale, but it hardly needs another telling. It is remarkable only for the gender of the protagonist. When a man kills his wife, he is a tortured rebel, *criminel de passion*, dusky Othello or bluff King Hal. When a woman kills her husband, she is never allowed to forget it. I stare at the drawing again. Alice Kyteler, four times widow in two dozen years, has evolved into a long-nailed monster, a Kilkenny Clytemnestra.

'Researching?'

My eyes swivel back to the bartender, who is polishing glasses with a Guinness tea towel. 'Beg your pardon?'

'Doing a radio programme or something? Family history?' she adds. Her hand has paused, knuckles yellow against the glass.

'More or less,' I tell her, with a ghost of a smile.

'Very nice.'

201

I glance back at the wall beside me, then at the others, weighted down with old maps and giant replica copper pots. No picture of Petronilla de Meath. I suppose I could ask the bartender, but I'm not sure if my mouth could bear to form the words.

Why is it that almost nobody knows Petronilla's name, when she was so much more remarkable than her mistress? No demon that Dame Alice called up and bound with spells ever served her so faithfully. What interests me is not so much the mistress's evil, which seems after almost seven centuries to amount to no more than a banal footnote in the annals of war and treachery, but the maid's extraordinary ordinariness. How through thick and thin, sickness and sin, Masses read backwards and Christian funerals, Petronilla retained her sense of being a good servant, whatever that could mean in a house like this one. As if she had heard some fireside tale that ended with the tag; *Whanne that yr mistresse sell here soule to Luciphere ond take a wisshe for to kille her lawfulle wedded husbandes, be you of gode cheere ond giff her al manere of aide for to brewe ye poysionne.*

'I love history, myself.'

I turn on the bartender, who is rubbing at the lipsticked rim of a glass. 'Why is that?'

Her blue eyes, behind her glasses, seem surprised by the question. 'Well, it makes you feel more complete, doesn't it?' A pause. 'Knowing where you're from, as it were.'

'Does it?'

'Reminds you there's more to the whole business than your own little life.' She gives me a wholly unmerited smile. 'I like to think that no one ever really dies as long as their folks remember them.'

'Perhaps they'd prefer to.'

'Remember them?'

'Prefer to die.'

'Oh. Oh I don't think so,' says the woman, as if to reassure us both.

I ask to be directed to the ladies; this seems the best excuse for poking around. For all the dark wood, most of these walls look new; these smooth beams have never had a sconce stuck in them. I hitch up my tights, careful not to tear them. I take off my heavy ring to wash my hands. My face looks back at me with a hint of defiance: no new lines today. On the wall, a Kondo-Vend machine offers me a Quality Range of Luxury Lubricated Sheath Contraceptives. I can tell I won't find what I'm looking for in Kyteler's Inn.

As I cross the narrow elbow of St Kierán's Street, I find myself humming a tune, a very old one; I realise that it has been stuck in my head since Dublin. The words slide on to each other like water over worn rocks. Voice on anonymous voice, disciplined in melancholy resignation.

> *Quiconques veut d'amors joïr*
> *Doit avoir foy et esperance*

Such patience the singers had back then, giving every melancholic syllable its own line of music, a full half-minute to a phrase, as if they had all the time in the world. *The seeker of love must have faith and hope*. Faith to keep you longing, hope to relieve your despair.

The town has become a maze of gift shops and boutiques; I can't tell where anything used to be. As I step off a kerb, a car roars by, inches from my handbag. *Labhair Gaeilge*, says the bumper sticker, as if simple encouragement to *Speak Irish* could set my tongue to talking the language I've long forgotten.

What was Petronilla's first name, I wonder? The one she knew herself by when she was a raw serving-maid who could speak only two tongues and both of them with a County Meath accent. When her hair still fell loose under her white coif, not yet having been tucked away as the mark of womanhood. When she came in a cart to Kilkenny, telling her beads, before her mistress renamed her for the saint whose day it was, the Roman Virgin who tended Peter: Petronilla. What went through the girl's head those first months, I wonder, as she ran to order: 'Fetch my Venetian brocade, the rayed one you fool,' or 'Strap on my pattens if you would not have me wade through every puddle in town,' or (in a low voice) 'Have you fetched candles of beeswax for the ceremony?'

Petronilla was Dame Alice's loyal bondswoman from the start; she was a dagger thrown back and forward between those ruby-weighted hands. The first Sabbath made her retch in a corner, but she said nothing, told no one, never broke trust. The girl had no malice of her own, but her mistress's orders girded her like chain mail, and obedience made her brave.

The most inexplicable thing is that at no point in her eventual imprisonment and trial did Petronilla try to run away. Did she keep hoping Dame Alice would return from England to burst the doors, with all the force of law or simply a click of her stained fingers? Or did the maid simply keep her garbled faith, offering herself as ransom for her vanished mistress, waiting on the pleasure of the dark master? Or, more likely, did some portion of her drugged conscience feel her execution to be a proper end to the story?

What is clear is that she was not one of the weeping, piteous victims who flock across the pages of history. She embraced her death as a final order. Does that make her mistress's betrayal better or worse? All the records have to say on the matter is that at the hour of her death, Petronilla declared that Dame Alice was the most powerful witch in the world.

I feel slightly faint. I am standing on a street corner with a slightly crazed expression. A small girl leaning against a lamp-post watches me; she has a purple birthmark the shape of a kidney. 'Lights changed ages ago, Mrs,' she points out.

I cross, without answering her. I should be looking for the gaol, but I can't face it yet. I wander up the hill, past Dunnes Stores, a stall selling local fudge, a poster inviting costumed revellers to a Quentin Tarantino Night.

St Canices's seems almost small after the great cathedrals of England. Its walls are grey and serene; beside it, the round tower pencils the clouds. I look for the grave, but they must have moved it. Inside the church I finally stumble across the headstone, one of a dozen propped against the walls. With difficulty I make out the old French letters framing a *fleur de lys* cross. *Here lies José de Keteller*, they say. *Say thou who passest here a prayer*.

José de Keteller came to this town in chain mail with a long sword, I remember, an old-style legitimate killer. Learned Gaelic, grew long moustaches, finally even rode without a saddle in the native way. A peaceful settler, shaping himself to the island on which fate had placed him, he was hardly to know how his surname would be immortalised by his iron-willed daughter. Why is it so much worse to execute husbands than infidels, I wonder? Most of us are descended from killers, one way or another.

None of this is telling me anything I didn't already know, and my ankles are beginning to ache. In the Museum, I take my shoes off for a moment to stretch my feet on the smooth wooden floor. What a motley collection we have here: grisset and candle-mould, cypress chest and footstool, a copy of a will specifying what a certain widow would inherit from her husband if she did not remarry or have carnal knowledge of any man willingly (this last bit makes me smile), and an ancient deer skull with antlers six feet wide. On a dusty shelf I find huge metal tongs, for stamping IHS on holy wafers. My heart begins to thump again.

Downstairs in the bookshop, I calm myself with a collection of photographs of Irish lakes. The girl assesses me as a browser, and turns back to the phone, demanding (in an accent that I have not heard in a long time) to know who said she'd said she fancied that spotty eejit. I turn the pages, recognising the heads of birds. I move on to the small history shelf, where I learn that the town's most famous witch was, in fact, framed.

'Alice Kyteler (possibly a misspelling of Kettle, a fairly common English surname),' I read in one hardback,

> was a victim of a combination of the worst excesses of fourteenth-century Christo-patriarchy. Threatening to men by virtue of her emotional and financial independence, this irrepressible *bourgeoise*, who always kept her maiden name through repeated widowhoods, aroused the hostility of avaricious relatives and a misogynistic Catholic establishment. As in so many other 'witch trials', powerful men (both church and lay) projected their own unconscious fantasies of sexual/satanic perversion onto the blank canvas of a woman's life.

I can't help smiling: *blank canvas*, my eye. There is a grain of truth there, of course: before she ever trafficked with darkness, the citizens of Kilkenny resented the Kyteler woman's fine house, bright gowns, every last ruby on her fingers. But that hardly makes her innocent.

The girl on the phone is eyeing me wearily. She is letting her friend speak now, the faraway voice winding down like clockwork.

How the late twentieth century loves to issue general pardons. At this distance, it cannot distinguish the rare cases of serious evil from those of farmers' wives burnt by neighbourly malice. Dame Alice should not be lumped in with the victims. She was the real thing. She could be said to have deserved the punishment she never got.

Unlike Petronilla de Meath, not mentioned in the historical analysis. Petronilla, who should have been set free when the whole sorry mess was concluded. Why could she not have been shaken out like a wide-eyed cat from a sack, to run across country and live some ordinary life?

It is too hot in here, all at once; too cosy, with a tub of Connemara Marble Worry Stones going cheap beside the till, and remaindered Romance stacked high on a table between the symmetrical stares of Décor and Archaeology. I replace the books neatly and leave.

Outside it is cooler, at least; the edgy breeze of late afternoon fills the town of Kilkenny. I walk along the main shopping street, wondering where the gaol could have got to. A hamburger carton impales itself on my heel; I kick it off. My toes feel crushed; my head is beginning to pound. Anything could have been built on the site of Petronilla's last months: a hardware shop, a B&B, a public toilet. A gaol is by nature anonymous; all it requires is four walls or a hole in the ground, a barred square of light if you're lucky.

I pause outside a pub offering Live Trad To-Nite. I stare at the five narrow bars just above ground level, the darkness behind them. All they hide is a cellar of beer barrels, but if I close my eyes I can almost see her pallid hands caressing the iron. Petronilla in the shadows, crouched in her dirty smock, once good linen, a present after her first year of service. A face like a drop of honey, looking out of a bedraggled wimple – unless they shamed her by leaving her head naked. Did her pale hair come down at last, escaping coif and cap and veil, falling back into girlhood?

I rest my palms against the pub's grey slate, ignoring the glances of passers-by, and try to conjure up the rest of her. Would there be marks of torture, the telltale insignia on wrists and soles? Probably not; there would have been no need, since she seems to have told the whole story freely once her mistress had escaped to safety. Besides, they probably preferred to bring the girl unmarked to the stake, a perfect sacrifice to the fire-breathing dragon. Where would they have done it, I wonder – outside the gaol, outside the city walls, or in the busy thoroughfare of the market square? Which supermarket sits on Petronilla's ashes now? Pressing my fingertips so hard against the cement that they turn grey, I ask every question I can think of. Was there anyone there that day who, remembering alms or a kind word or just the turn of her cheek, had enough mercy on the girl to add wet faggots to the kindling? Was there enough smoke to put her to sleep before flames licked the arches of her feet?

This is one of the times when I wish I still had the ability to cry.

Petronilla is not here. There is nothing left. I do not know what I was hoping for, exactly: some sign of presence, some message scratched for me on the prison wall, some whisper from her walking ghost. I shut my eyes more tightly, but all I can hear is an inane pop song leaking from a taxi window. *Hold on*, the singer begs, *every word I say is true. Hold on, I'll be coming back for you.*

I let go of the wall; the pads of my fingers are scored and pock-marked. As I stare at them they plump into their usual shape. The daily miracle, the return to the same healthy flesh. How long must it go on?

I stride back to my car, through a crocodile of French schoolchildren; in the car park, I have some difficulty remembering what colour Volvo I rented. Automatically I fasten my seatbelt.

I have never tried to kill myself; I am afraid to discover that it would not work. I shrug off my shoes and lean my head back on the padded rest. What on earth am I doing here?

My ring is cutting into my finger; I pull it off and stare at it. Rubies to stave off disease; this is my last one. Once in Birmingham someone tried to mug me, and I cracked his nose with this ring.

Time has not absolved me of anything. The clothes have been transformed, the name is different – I change it every fifty years or so – but the face in the rear view mirror is the same. And in almost seven centuries of exile I have not managed to forget Petronilla.

It is almost funny, is it not? One would think that a woman who in her esoteric researches had stumbled across the secret of immortality would feel free. Exhausted by life's repetitions, yes, starved for fresh food, tormented by the bargain she made, but in some sense free. To wander, at least, to move, to leave behind the quarrels of mortals. I never expected to be so haunted by one face that I would have to make my way back to Kilkenny.

More than any husband or lover or child; more than anyone I have hurt since I went into exile; more than anyone I left without warning (when they wondered why I was not ageing) or killed with my bare hands (when they deserved it). Petronilla's is the only death I still regret. Leaving her behind was the worst thing I have ever done.

I did no harm to my first husband, the richest moneylender in Kilkenny; I bore him a son and fed him tidbits of roast rabbit on his deathbed. As for my second – in my grandmother's time I could have followed the old ways and left him after a year and a day, but under Common Law I was his for life, to stamp his mark on. I bent under his weight like a reed, and in the pool of humiliation I brushed against my power. He was sick already

209

– the beatings were getting feebler – but the poison sped him on. My third . . . yes, I remember. I despatched him in a night, after I caught him in the linen cupboard ripping the skirt off Petronilla. The night before his funeral I dropped his heart in the River Nore.

As for my fourth, John le Poer, he was a loving man who shut his ears to the rumours circulating about me. But by then, you must understand, I had signed with my own blood, and the sacrifice was called for. His hair came out in handfuls, when I brushed it at night; his nails began to bend backwards. Petronilla never claimed to understand the rituals, but she knew that whatever Dame Alice said had to happen. When John, made suspicious at last by the gossip of my dead husbands' disinherited children, talked to Bishop Ledrede, it was my faithful maid, my flawless echo, who repeated to me every word they had said. When my husband wrenched the key from my belt and burst into my room, finding and forcing open the padlocked boxes, I kept one curious eye on Petronilla. She wept because the story was almost over, but she showed no shame.

I was charged along with eleven accomplices, most of whom barely knew me to see. The seven charges told of dogs torn limb from limb and scattered at crossroads, fornication with Ethiopian hobgoblins, and a dead baby's flesh boiled in a robber's skull. The grease I used to keep my face soft was listed as a sorcerous ointment for the staff on which I flew across Kilkenny town by night. Bishop Ledrede was widely read, and had a vivid imagination. He was not to know that power is composed of simple elements, once you have stumbled across it.

Ledrede did not prosecute me for the money his spiritual court could hope to confiscate; like myself, he was motivated by wrath and glory. And so, when I had indicted him for defamation and sailed to England with all my jewels, when my son William had agreed to pay for the reroofing of St Canice's as a penance, and when the other accused accomplices had melted into the night, then the Bishop focused his gaze on Petronilla. She was all he had left.

It was not that I could not have brought her with me, torn her out of prison somehow; I simply never thought to. That is my crime; that in the urgency of my flight, full of the sense of my own devilish importance, I did not even condemn my maid deliberately, but carelessly, as I might have said, 'Pick up that sarsenet gown.'

I have had plenty of time to think of her since. In almost seven centuries of wandering I can make an informed comparison: I have met no one who loved so well or was so betrayed. She was not a natural killer: she ground poisons together out of mute loyalty, and what purer motive is there than that?

It is so long since I have killed, I have almost forgotten how. It is not worth risking nowadays. They lock you up, take down what you say and never put an end to it. Oh Petronilla, how I envy your death. Not the manner of it, the pain and squalor, but its definition. How it took you by the hand and led you away before your bursting youth could dwindle.

Unless I am casting a web of glamour over the story to lessen my guilt? But that is not how it works. My envy and my guilt pin each other down. Petronilla's, short and powerless, is the life I did not lead, and cannot lead no matter how long I drag on, and will never fully understand. Petronilla's exultant face is the one I cannot leave behind me. She follows, just out of view, and all the rippling voices are hers.

Quiconques veut d'amors joïr
Doit avoir foy et esperance

211

Having had faith and hope enough to last her short lifetime, did it come down to love in the end? Was that what she feasted on, among the rats in Kilkenny gaol? How could I be loved by such as her?

For all my sheer elastic skin, I am a hollow woman. My ribs are an empty cauldron now; my breath couldn't put out a candle.

I start the car. My one faith is that I will find some trace of Petronilla. My one hope is that she will teach me how to die. My one love now, the only one whose face I can remember. There, around some corner, she burns, she burns.

Note

My main source for 'Looking for Petronilla' is the entry for 1323 in Raphaell Holinshed's *The Historie of Ireland* (1577). The Bishop of Ossory's Latin manuscript account of the trial was edited by Thomas Wright as *A Contemporary Narrative of the Proceedings Against Dame Alice Kyteler* (1843). A useful account of the case is found in St John Seymour's *Irish Witchcraft and Demonology* (1913, 1989). The song quoted is the anonymous rondeau, 'Quiconques Veut D'Amors Joïr', available on the Gothic Voices album, *The Medieval Romantics*.

Petronilla de Meath was burnt alive in Kilkenny 1324. Dame Alice is said to have escaped to England.